Ironside

The English King who fought the Danes

Fen Flack

Flack Publishing

Flack Books, 23 Stourport Road, Bewdley, Worcestershire DY12 1BB, UK

www.flackbooks.weebly.com

First edition 2016

The right of Fen Flack to be identified as the author of this work has been asserted by her in accordance with the Copyright, Designs and Patents Act 1988.

Cover design by Head Desk Graphic Design Studio from an illustration by Bhavin Mistry

Printed in the UK by A & G Printing Co. Ltd. of Stourport-on-Severn, Worcestershire DY13 9AX

ISBN 978-0-9564961-5-7

Characters

Clergy

Lyfing, Archbishop of Canterbury
Wulfstan, Archbishop of York and Bishop of Worcester
Ealdwine, one of Edmund's Chaplains
Aelfric, Abbot of Evesham
Alkmund, Chaplain to Eadric Streona
Aelfsige, Bishop of Winchester

The Danes

Swein
Cnut, his son
Thorkell the Tall

Others

Wulfgar, the young narrator
Aelfnoth, Athelstan's sword-polisher
Aelfmaer, Athelstan's seneschal/estate manager
Aelfwine, Athelstan's priest
Olaf Haraldson, a Norwegian

GLOSSARY

Aetheling – a son of the King, one of those considered worthy to succeed to the throne

Fyrd – a fighting force, raised locally

Heriot – a tax paid to the King, usually following someone's death

Niello – a decoration created by engraved grooves being filled with a black composition

Pallium – the part of an archbishop's robes that he receives from the Pope by visiting Rome and which gives him his authority

Reeve – a local official, sheriff is a corruption of "shire reeve"

Relics – objects associated with saints, often thought to have miraculous powers

Seax – short sword

Seneschal – manager of an estate

Shrived – the result of confession of sin followed by receiving assurance from a priest that God has forgiven

Thegn (pronounced thane) – a lord, of lower rank than an earl

Weregild – payment made by a criminal to those against whom he committed the crime

Witan – the King's council, which included bishops, earls and thegns

Royal Family Tree

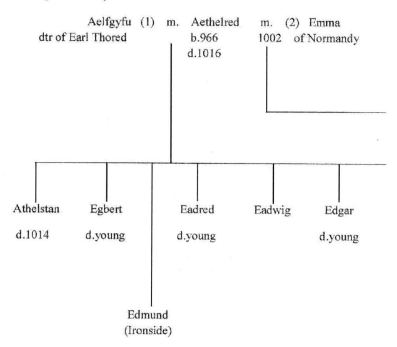

Aelfgyfu (1)   m.   Aethelred   m.   (2)   Emma
dtr of Earl Thored   b.966   1002   of Normandy
                             d.1016

Athelstan   Egbert   Eadred   Eadwig   Edgar

d.1014   d.young   d.young   d.young

Edmund
(Ironside)

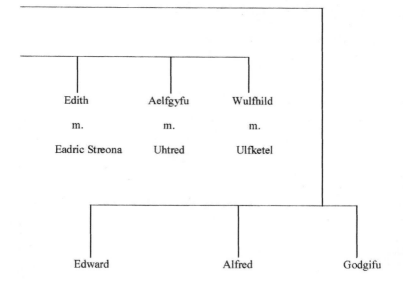

Edith
m.
Eadric Streona

Aelfgyfu
m.
Uhtred

Wulfhild
m.
Ulfketel

Edward

Alfred

Godgifu

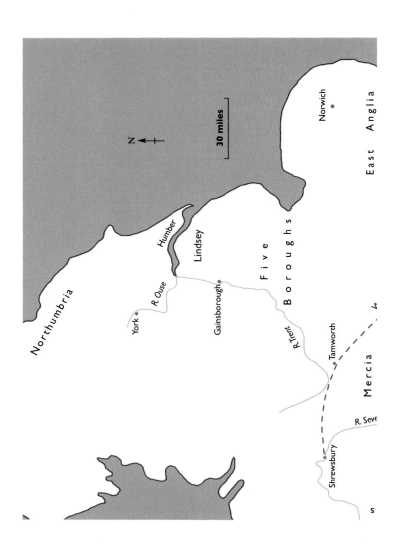

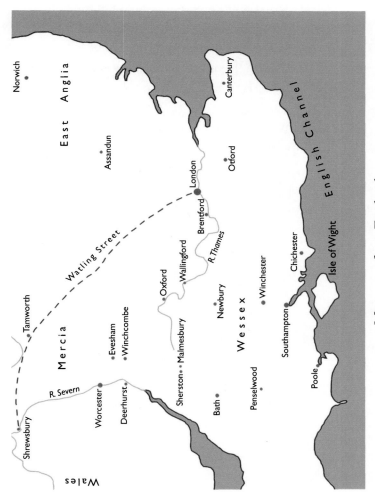

Map of England

The book could not have been done without the help of:

The ACW group in Leamington Spa, Judy Bennett,
Bewdley Bards, Bishop's Wood Educational Centre,
Birmingham Central Library, Jill Cainey, Dr. Chris
Callow, Andrew and Susie Crang, Professor Christopher
Dyer, the Revd Nigel Feaver Vicar of Wincanton and
Pen Selwood, Louise Flack for help with the Derbyshire
dialect, Martin Flegg for the map, Michael Hare,
Margaret Hawkins, Janey Hewett, Fran Hill, Dr.
Andrew Hopper, The Hive at Worcester, Ali and Sarah
Hull, Liz Munslow for proofreading and support, Geoff
Parcell, John Rhymer, Somerset Archaeological Service,
Richard Stancomb, Professor Joanna Story, Æd
Thompson of The Thanes of Mercia, Ben Williams, the
David Wilson Library at the University of Leicester and
Wiltshire Archaeological Service

CHAPTER 1

There are those moments when you hear a piece of news and the world freezes.

It was Lammas in the year of Our Lord 1013 and we were visiting the ealdorman Siferth at his home in Derbyshire. I was ten and had only recently joined the aetheling's household, my uncle (the King's butler) having secured the post for me. My lord Edmund was then about 24, his face tanned and his fair hair bleached by the sun. I thought him a handsome man to serve and was pleased by my good fortune. Also, I was beginning to discover how often he travelled, accepting hospitality from the King's thegns and keeping abreast of all that was happening around the country. We had been in Derbyshire since mid July.

"Wulfgar, more mead."

I hurried to fill my lord's cup as he feasted.

The air was still, almost stifling, the way it is at the end of a hot day. There was no lit hearth in the hall that evening. They had cooked the fish and meat on a fire made in the yard – a sweltering job, but at least free of midges. The table was strewn with sprigs of balm mixed with flowers of meadowsweet and there was tansy too, to discourage the flies, but they still buzzed round the food.

The timber-framed hall with its thick thatch was filled with men, earl Siferth's household and my lord's retainers too. The windows were unshuttered and the door left open, but even so, the smell of sweat and mead hung unmoving.

My lord Edmund, wearing a thin dun tunic and no leggings (because of the heat), sat at the main table next to earl Siferth's wife. The earl was broad of shoulders and rotund, wearing his hair long and his beard uncut. He was engrossed in eating and telling jokes to his men, so he left the lady Frida to entertain their guest.

She was much younger than her husband, or so I thought. Her gown was harebell blue and matched her eyes. Her eyebrows were sandy, suggesting that golden hair was hidden under her headdress. I thought her pretty.

"They are discontented, that I know," she told my lord.

He raised his eyebrows by way of query.

"The King, they believe, has not judged wisely," she added.

"Indeed, my father surrounds himself with poor counsellors," my lord commented.

"Like the earl of Mercia?"

"Eadric? Though he's married to Edith, I don't like him. He kills too easily and has rightly earned the name Streona, the acquisitor, for he keeps adding to his holding of land."

"They would back your brother."

My lord frowned.

"Careful what you say," he whispered, not meeting her eye. "Such talk is dangerous. Athelstan cannot be king until my father dies – and hastening his death would be treason."

"But there is talk your father wishes the aetheling Edward to be his heir."

My lord grunted. "If my stepmother had her way, her children would take precedence. It may even be that my father agreed to that when he married her, but we shall see. Edward is but a boy of eight. Our country needs a strong ruler, a man who can fight the Danes. Athelstan will do that well."

"But there is so much discontent up north that I fear for the future – that ... ." She stopped.

"Voice your fears. You can trust me." He had turned to gaze at her troubled face.

"They may even welcome a Danish lord," she breathed.

"Never! Your lord would not agree, surely?"

"My lord Siferth follows his brother."

There was a commotion in the doorway of the hall and a red-faced messenger ran in, sweat weeping from every pore.

"My lord!" he gasped. "The Danes are at Gainsborough!"

My lord Edmund leapt up.

"Have the lords called out the fyrd?" he cried.

The messenger turned his shocked face to him, but said nothing.

"Come on, man!" shouted earl Siferth. "What's the

3

rest of your news? Is there a call to mobilise?"

"No." There was a horrible pause. Even I sensed something was badly wrong. "All the northern lords have submitted to Swein and his son Cnut. Even your brother earl Morcar."

The only sound was the barking of a dog that had been disturbed by the interruption.

"God preserve us," my lord said, almost to himself. "I must ride south to my father."

"I'm so sorry." The lady Frida had her hand on his arm. "I'm so very sorry."

He took her hand and lifted it to his lips.

"I know," he said quietly. "Your lord will follow his brother. I pray you will be kept safe." His eyes were fixed on her anxious face. "And I pray we will meet again. Wulfgar, prepare to leave."

I thought he would have stayed holding her, gazing at her, but suddenly he pulled away. While he paid his respects to earl Siferth and no doubt thanked him for his hospitality, I was off to round up our party and help get provisions for the journey.

The long summer day gave us good light for travelling, and a clear sky lit by a plump moon meant we could see our way through the night. My lord had decided simply to take me and three of his men while the rest were to follow. Thus we could travel fast, for our news was urgent.

As I was a skinny lad, I sat in front of my lord on his

horse and sometimes we could talk.

"How did the Danes get to Gainsborough?" I asked.

"There was news their fleet had been sighted," my lord replied, "but off Essex. It seems Swein has brought his ships north and come up the Humber."

"Is Gainsborough on the coast?"

"No, it is well inland, up the River Trent."

"Then that's serious?"

"Yes. The north has given in quickly. Too quickly." His tone was grim.

"Didn't they fight?" I wanted to know.

"It seems not. I don't like it. It's almost as though the northern lords were expecting him and had agreed to stand back."

"And now?" I asked.

"I guess he'll move south, against Mercia."

"Earl Eadric will fight, won't he?"

"I should hope so! But he's a rat. I'm never sure what he'll do next."

I was puzzled for I knew the Danes had come before, but we'd always fought them – or tried to.

"I don't understand," I confessed. "Why did the northern lords give in so easily?"

My lord was quiet and I remembered his conversation with the lady Frida. The words "discontent" and "unwise judgments" came to mind.

"My father hasn't been wise in his treatment of them," he said at last. "Earl Aelfhelm of Northumbria was murdered. Eadric organised it, but we all know my father wanted it. And then the sons were blinded, so that they could not succeed to his earldom. Earl Morcar is married to earl Aelfhelm's niece."

I sensed a bleak future. We had only managed to keep the Danes from overrunning us by fighting together and then paying them off. If the northern part of the kingdom had now decided to stand back and see if the king crumpled without them, then we were in deep trouble.

We made good time to London and went straight to the royal residence, only to find King Aethelred wasn't there. The court, we were told, was at Canterbury. So we found fresh horses, crossed the Thames by the bridge near Southwark and pushed on into Kent.

The King was receiving hospitality from Archbishop Lyfing and we found them deep in conversation.

"My lord, I bring grave news," my lord Edmund declared, briefly kneeling before his father.

The King looked up. It was the first time I had seen him at such close quarters and I was stunned at how old he looked. He was clean-shaven, had medium-length grey hair, a sallow complexion and sunken cheeks. His brow wore a permanent furrow, I was soon to discover.

"Edmund! I thought you'd gone north."

"I had. I was staying at the household of earl Siferth in Derbyshire when a messenger came with news of a Danish invasion."

"Invasion? They've landed somewhere? Do you

mean they have done more than raid some coastal settlements?"

"They're in Gainsborough."

"Gainsborough! Oh, God, no!"

The King put his hands over his eyes as though being unable to see would take away the terrible image.

"It's worse than that," my lord Edmund continued. "We hear the northern lords have submitted to Swein and his son Cnut."

"Oh, God, no! No!"

I thought the King might break down weeping.

"My lord, do not despair," the Archbishop sought to encourage him. "We must trust in God. He has sent this as a test."

"Some have already failed the test of loyalty," my lord Edmund said sharply.

The King looked at him now.

"Who has submitted?" he asked and I detected a tremor of fear in his voice.

"Earl Morcar of the Five Boroughs, and his brother Siferth will follow suit. The lords of York and Lindsey."

My lord Edmund paused.

"And?" the King whispered.

"It is believed earl Ulfketel has too, which means East Anglia is under Danish control."

"Does it mean nothing to Ulfketel that I gave him Wulfhild in marriage?" The King was now beginning to get angry. "And Uhtred?"

"There was no news of earl Uhtred," his son replied, "but I fear he may have no option but to submit, for Swein holds all the land between us and him."

"Where is their loyalty?" the King raged.

"They have to be pragmatic," my lord suggested. "They have to consider their homes and their people. These are good men faced with hard choices."

"And you, you and your brother Athelstan, are too friendly with them," the king accused.

"And you are not friendly enough," my lord rejoined. "These men need cultivating, not condemning. Your policies have driven them into the arms of the Danes!"

"How dare you say that!"

The King leapt up and hit my lord across the face with his hand. The Archbishop leapt up too.

"My lord! Stay your hand! These are difficult times."

"Made worse by our fighting each other." My lord had stepped back instinctively, perhaps anticipating another blow.

"Indeed," the Archbishop agreed. "We must put past mistakes behind us and find a way of meeting this challenge together."

"Past mistakes?" the King shouted.

It was now the Archbishop's turn to step back.

"I only meant, my lord, that there may have been some things that are now regretted."

"Like?"

"Like the death of earl Aelfhelm," my lord Edmund interrupted.

"He was a traitor," declared the King. "If I regret anything it is that I have trusted Uhtred and Ulfketel with my daughters." He sat down and looked around. "Where's Eadric?" he demanded. "At least I can trust him."

The Archbishop glanced at my lord and I wondered if he too had a low opinion of the earl of Mercia. A servant scurried from the room.

"The court should return to London," said my lord Edmund.

He had clenched his fists tight. I guessed he was trying hard to control his frustration.

"Well, Lyfing, it doesn't look as though you'll be making that journey to Rome just yet," the King commented. "You'll have to manage as best you can and let Wulfstan continue to act as archbishop for both York and Canterbury. There are far more pressing needs – like stopping those damned Danes from harrying us further."

The King was up again. He stalked away from us, calling for his bodyguard. I was stunned by his sudden mood changes.

"I'll get my servants to give you some food," the Archbishop told us. "You've had a long – and difficult journey."

"We thank you for your hospitality," my lord replied.

So my lord and his followers, me included, found

ourselves sharing a meal of bread and fish; he didn't insist on eating separately.

"Do you know, Wulfgar, what happened to the last Archbishop of Canterbury?" my lord asked me.

My mouth was full of food, so I shook my head.

"The Danes were ravaging in Kent in the autumn, nearly two years ago," he told me, "and besieged Canterbury."

I looked around and noticed for the first time that the building we were in was fairly new.

"The city resisted," my lord continued, "but there was a traitor in their midst and he told the enemy how to get in. The Danes burned a lot of the buildings and took many people prisoner. They kept them for ransom purposes. The rich, the important – they thought to get money in exchange for their lives."

He took a mouthful of food and I had to wait while he chewed the coarse bread and washed it down with ale.

"One of the prisoners was the Archbishop," he went on, "a saintly man called Aelfheah. They wanted a huge amount of money for him, but he knew how poor his people were and he wouldn't let them pay it."

"More fool him," muttered one of our group.

"He was a godly man, putting others before himself," responded another of the diners.

"Wanted to be a saint more like," replied the first man.

Their comments allowed my lord to continue eating. At last, he completed his tale.

"There was no money forthcoming even after several months and the Danes ... when? Easter 1012 ... they were having a feast – gnawing on ox bones and drinking too much strong wine – and, well, they battered him to death with the bones."

I stopped eating.

"That's awful!" I cried.

"That's the Danes for you," was his answer. "Though something good came out of it. A Dane called Thorkell the Tall, and I can tell you he *is* tall, he was disgusted by the actions of his fellow Danes and decided to change sides. So now we have a powerful Danish warlord fighting for us, together with his 45 ships – at a price, of course."

"Will he stop Swein?" I asked.

"Who knows. He may not be too happy to fight his former lord. If a man changes sides, he can find himself killing his friends."

I chewed on my bread and wondered about the world we lived in. How did you know who your friend was? The next day he might be your enemy. And one day your enemies might be your friends. In my innocence, I thought all men should be loyal to their lord, whatever happened. But I was learning that others disagreed.

CHAPTER 2

We all returned to London. The blazing sun did nothing to raise our spirits, rather it left us listless and despondent with no zest for the task ahead. But action there had to be.

The King's men were despatched around the city to check the defences and ensure there were armed men to guard any weak points. My lord Edmund also went about, talking to the citizens, listening and encouraging them, while the King himself sat brooding in his hall.

"The defences are looking good, my lord," the aetheling reported to his father. "I've also made enquiries about supplies of food and there is plenty at present because of the recent good harvest."

I was sitting quietly by, polishing his sword. His brother Athelstan had a sword-polisher in his household; his name was Aelfnoth and he had shown me what to do, as I was meant to be learning all the tasks done by an aetheling's retainers. I liked sword-polishing as it meant my ears were free to listen in on conversations – for I was invisible to these great men.

"So if Swein gets this far, we'll hold out, you think," the King muttered.

"Yes, I believe so, but he could be stopped." My lord turned as the earl of Mercia appeared.

I had heard something of this man, Eadric the Greedy they called him. Well over thirty I reckoned, broad and muscular with raven-black hair and eyes too close together, almost hidden by thick eyebrows. Yet he was the King's favourite, a man who could do no wrong.

"My lord Eadric, I thought you would have returned to Mercia," was my lord Edmund's comment.

"My place is by the King," was his response. "Leofwine can raise the fyrd as he leads the Hwicce. My people are too far west."

"That depends on Swein's route south," my lord responded. "We can't be sure he'll come directly south against London. He may seek submission from other areas first."

"He'll come here," the earl declared. "I don't doubt that and we can match him – with our forces and those of Thorkell. We can send him back up north."

He sounded very confident, perhaps a bit too confident, but it was this sort of talk that the King liked, as it made him feel less gloomy. Indeed, I saw a light of hope in his eyes.

"It won't be that easy," my lord warned.

When I took the sword to Aelfnoth for his inspection, I asked him what he thought.

"It's difficult to predict," he began. "Swein seems to have a strong grip on all the territory north of Watling Street, the old boundary with the Danes."

"I've heard the country used to be split," I commented, "but that was long ago, wasn't it?"

"In the time of our greatest king, Alfred. He had been pushed into the marshes of Somerset over a hundred years ago, but he won a battle with the Danes and the land was divided." Aelfnoth smiled. "But not for long. His heirs pushed the foreigners back bit by bit."

"If the Danes have done it before, then surely they can do it again," I suggested.

Aelfnoth glanced around before he answered.

"Our King has bad counsellors," he whispered. "And some valuable resources have been lost unnecessarily. Like the matter of the ships – that was a farce!"

"Tell me about it," I begged.

"It was four years ago, when the King ordered many ships to be built to secure our coast. And many were. There was a formidable fleet moored at Sandwich. Then there was trouble. You've probably met earl Eadric."

I nodded.

"He had a brother Brihtric, who accused another lord, one Wulfnoth, of some foul deed. But the King did not call them both to him to settle the matter. Perhaps Wulfnoth feared he'd get no justice, seeing who his accuser was."

Aelfnoth winked and I understood. The King would inevitably favour Eadric's brother.

"So this Wulfnoth took twenty of these ships and went off raiding along the south coast."

"That's crazy!" I responded.

"Even crazier was Brihtric's response. He took *eighty* ships and chased him. But the weather intervened and Brihtric's ships were cast ashore in a storm. Wulfnoth was a better sailor. He avoided the storm, but took advantage of his enemy's plight and burned the stranded ships. So that way the King lost *a hundred* ships."

"No wonder we can't keep the Danish fleet at bay," was my response.

"We lost a good commander in Wulfnoth for he disappeared into exile and we lost Brihtric too, for he dared not show his face at court again. Even his brother was angry at the mess he'd made."

I was despondent that day, partly through hearing of our failures in the recent past and partly through being told I'd only done half a job in polishing the sword. I could do something about the sword, but nothing about the marauding Danes – except be there for my lord and do my best to serve him well.

My lord Edmund was out and about every day, anxious and restless, though trying not to show he was. But I could tell, for he rarely sat down for long, and even when the court met together to eat each evening, he was not always present or didn't stay long. In times of peace, these would be good occasions, opportunities to tell tales and riddles and relax over horns of mead. But now there was merely subdued conversation, all of us wondering what was happening.

News was coming in – slowly – brought by messengers, hot and dusty after a hurried journey. So we knew Swein was on the move and we heard there was no destruction or fighting until he crossed Watling Street, that old divide. So Leicester and Northampton had been spared. It was beyond Towcester that there had been resistance – ineffective it seemed.

What was most worrying was that Swein's route appeared to be towards Oxford rather than London.

"My lord, why haven't we sent an army against the Danes?" I asked.

The aetheling shrugged his shoulders.

"The men of London will only fight to defend their city," he explained. "It's difficult to get them to see beyond their walls. We raise a local army, a fyrd."

"Each shire raises its own?" I asked.

"Yes, it's done on an area basis, either by the King or the local earl. A shire or a region is called upon to provide men."

"So the King could raise a force to stop Swein?"

"He could." My lord paused. "But he does not choose to. He hopes his thegns will block the enemy's path." He gave me wry smile. "The king's sons have no authority. To be an aetheling simply means to be throneworthy. When a king dies, the Witan chooses the one best qualified for the task of ruling."

Talking of aethelings, it was there in London that I first met my lord's brothers. Athelstan was the oldest and I thought he looked like his father, somewhat lean, almost gaunt, but he was taller than my lord, his hair the colour of mud. My uncle, who had served the King for many years, told me that this aetheling was the King's particular favourite and had been raised by his grandmother, the lady Aelfthryth, whose reputation was formidable. It was whispered, but never spoken aloud, that she had arranged the death of Edward, our King's half-brother, so that her own son might take the throne. That was some thirty odd years ago. She was long since dead, as was the aethelings' mother, for the king now had a second wife and a second family.

I also met a young brother Eadwig. He was but a youth, not even twenty and the very image of my lord Athelstan. It seemed only my lord Edmund had his mother's features. I heard she had come from the far north, the daughter of a Northumbrian earl.

The King had daughters too, but none were at court as most were married. Even the one married to earl Eadric was not in London and I presumed she was somewhere in Mercia, at one of his many holdings. If he thought she would be safe there, he was in for a shock.

I also saw the two half-brothers, their sister and their mother. Edward was about eight and had a permanent look on his face as though he could smell something nasty. Alfred and Godgifu were younger, boisterous and noisy, cared for by nurses. Their mother was a woman to be reckoned with, imperious and aloof. She'd married the King when she was very young, but was now in her twenties and asserting herself. Frequently, I noticed her pushing Edward forward, making sure he sat next to the King. The King liked him, for he was only a child and didn't talk of things of state, though he was hardly a bundle of fun.

In these difficult times, the safest plan was to have the court together in a secure location – and London was just that. How vulnerable other parts of the country were, we were only beginning to discover.

Several days had passed since we had news Swein had crossed the old Roman road of Watling Street, and the whole city was tense. My lord couldn't rest – he would be at the walls looking north and questioning every trader who came in from that direction. One evening he had been persuaded to sit and eat with the court and I was near with a jug of ale to refill his cup if needed.

"News, my lord!" A servant ran into the hall. "A messenger has come from Oxford. He's just dismounting."

A dishevelled rider, covered in dust from the tracks, hurried in and knelt before the King.

"The Danes have ravaged Oxford!" he panted. "We fought hard, but they were too strong for us."

Earl Eadric leapt up, his pinched face devoid of colour, his hand gripping his cup.

"Is it lost?" he gasped.

"Yes and hostages have been given."

The earl's hand began to shake and he slammed down the cup, spilling some of the liquid.

"Wasn't Leofwine there to defend the town?" he demanded.

"Earl Leofwine was there and with a considerable force he'd gathered, but the Danes were too strong."

"Oh, God!" The King's hands grasped his wispy hair. "Oh, God! They have the north and now they have the Midlands."

"Is there any information on where they're heading next?" my lord Edmund asked.

"None, my lord," the messenger replied. "I had difficulty getting away on a horse. I thought you should know about Oxford."

"Yes, of course." My lord signalled to a servant. "Make sure this man and his horse receive due care."

All this news did was make the whole court even more despondent than it had been. Oxford was an important place and to lose it was a kick in the stomach. Earl Eadric blamed earl Leofwine and the King condoned this view. Was it only me who thought the earl of Mercia should have been there himself to lead the opposition? I suspected others thought so too, but dared not voice their thoughts. I noticed my lord deep in conversation with his older brother, but I couldn't hear what they said.

Surely London would be next to feel the fury of the Danes.

"Swein means to rule the land," my lord told me the next day. "This is no booty raid. He wants power."

"Can't we buy him off?" I asked. "That's worked in the past."

"I fear not. Why should he go away with some of our

money when he can stay and have all the resources of our land at his disposal?"

There was a horrid logic in that, which made me fear for the future. But I was not alone in my fear.

Most of us thought the Danes would turn south-east and come next against London. There was a quiet tension in the city, as people spoke in low tones and walked with hunched shoulders. Then our spies brought news that Swein was on the move again (having secured Oxford and east Mercia) and was heading ... south!

"Where's he going?" I asked my lord.

"My guess is Winchester," he answered. "He wants to secure Wessex. Then only London and the south-east is left to conquer."

"Who is there to defend Winchester?"

"Wessex is traditionally the king's own area," he explained, "but there are leaders there who will call out the fyrd and try to keep the enemy at bay."

I couldn't sense any optimism in his voice or in others I listened to. I wondered if even earl Eadric himself was beginning to panic, though he showed no outward signs and kept assuring the King that London could not fall. But if Swein were to hold all the rest of England, what would be the advantage of being holed up in a strong citadel?

In this period of waiting, we continued to get in supplies from the country. All those inside the walls should be safe and well-fed. As for those outside ... God help them! For they could be at the mercy of the marauders, who were men not renowned for showing mercy.

When the news finally came, I don't think anyone was really surprised. Winchester had followed Oxford. There had been resistance, but the Danes were too strong and now the main town in Wessex, its beating heart, was controlled by the enemy.

The King was in a deep gloom, while the Queen railed at him for being so weak. Earl Eadric felt her biting tongue as well.

"There'll be no mercy for us," she declared. "Our deaths will give Swein complete control. And don't think you'll be saved, Eadric. He'll have you for breakfast."

It was almost a relief when we finally saw the enemy forces approaching London. The waiting was over, the fighting could begin. The countryside around the city had been deserted as folk fled inside the walls for protection, leaving their homes to be burned if Swein so chose.

The Danes gathered on the north bank of the Thames and sent a messenger requesting surrender. Of course, that was rejected and we fired arrows from the walls into their camp.

By "we" I mean the mature and able-bodied men amongst us. I had been learning to use a bow, but I didn't yet have the strength to fire an arrow any real distance. I marvelled at what these older men could do. To some arrows, they fixed burning balls of straw and some of these landed on enemy tents and caused fires. The enemy retaliated in similar fashion, but we were ready with buckets of water to dowse any flames. They soon retreated beyond our range.

The arrow-firing only lasted for a short period and soon the Danes were staring at our defences and we were staring back – an uneasy stalemate. We weren't going the way of Oxford and Winchester.

"We did a bit of damage last night," my lord informed me, with a rare smile. "Under cover of darkness, a small group of our men slipped out of the city, skirted round the Danes and found some slack guards, whose throats they cut."

"But what difference will that make?" I asked.

"Just aggravation and a bit of demoralisation," he admitted. "It's a message: we're not submitting."

On another occasion, some cattle were moved out of the city and loosed in an area where the Danes might see them. But we had men hiding in the bushes and when a few of the enemy thought it safe to catch a cow, they found themselves attacked and killed.

These were mere trifles though. Swein could spare some of his force. Our puny attempts were no more than the irritation caused by a midge bite. In fact, that was probably their biggest problem – they were camped near marshy ground and the midges were breeding rapidly in the late summer heat.

If Swein hoped we would send out an army to fight him in the open, he was disappointed. We knew that could be our downfall.

"We have learned from our mistakes," my lord told me, "that we must not give an inch. There was a great battle, just over twenty years ago at Maldon – that's north of here, in Essex. The Danes were one side of a causeway and our forces the other. Our leader Byrhtnoth believed his force could overwhelm the Danes in a fair fight, so he let them cross the causeway and line up for a straight battle."

"Did he beat them?"

"No. He died and there was a terrible loss of life." My lord shook his head. "We should have enticed them over the causeway a few at a time and picked them off rather than allowing the whole force over. Fighting the Danes is not simply a matter of brute force; we need tactics."

I suspected my lord Edmund was behind a tactic that was tried out the next day. News travelled through the city that a force of our men had approached the Danes but from the south and therefore were the other side of the Thames. They shouted across at the enemy and taunted them. That stretch of the river looked benign and shallow, so some Danes, well, quite a lot by the sound of it, tried to ford the river to have a fight. But the river was more hazardous than they realised and some of them fell into deep pits hidden under the murky water, while others stumbled over hidden objects, I think put there by us. Before long, the river was full of men, weighed down with weapons, struggling to cross. The English laughed at them. The few who got across were soon cut down, so those behind tried to retreat. Our forces watched as men drowned.

The number who died was not huge, but again it was a demoralising situation, one aimed at showing our enemies how inept they were.

The effect was unexpected.

CHAPTER 3

My lord was unusually quiet that evening as we ate together in the great hall. There was even laughter, not a common sound at the time. They were recounting tales of Danes slipping and being unable to get up because the water had lodged in their clothing.

"We let the river do its work," boasted one man. "There was hardly any need to fight."

My lord was not joining in the banter and I wondered for a moment if he regretted the loss of life, though we all knew our enemies would not regret our men being drowned. At last, I caught his eye and he gave me the smallest of smiles.

Ah! I thought. You were behind this.

The next morning he had me go with him to stand looking over the walls.

"What do you see, Wulfgar?"

"The enemy's camp."

"Yes, but what are they doing?"

I screwed up my eyes to focus more intently, as the Danes were a good way off.

"They are going about their business as usual," I said at length. "Checking their horses and their weapons."

"I think they are doing something more," he replied. "I have watched them every morning and they are behaving differently today."

"Are they?"

I looked again. I concentrated very hard, but I knew he had the advantage over me.

"Oh, they are packing things!" I cried, and to verify my observation, a tent was taken down as we gazed. "Are they leaving?"

"I think so."

"That's wonderful! We've won!"

He shook his head.

"No, we have held firm, but we haven't won."

He would say no more, but the news brought jubilation to the streets of London, and people smiled for the first time in weeks. I kept checking as the day progressed and by just after midday, the Danes had gone, though no one was venturing out of the security of the walls just yet in case it was a trap. We would wait to hear what our spies told us about the whereabouts of the enemy. But for now we could rejoice.

Again, however, my lord was quiet and did not join in the laughter.

"I said we would withstand them," declared earl Eadric, glowing as though he had personally performed a 'David', and killed Goliath. "They've gone with their tails between their legs."

"London has won," the King added. "Soon we shall hear they've retreated to their ships in the Humber."

The next morning we were back looking over the walls, but there was only a scene of peace before us, with not a Dane in sight.

"Wulfgar, if you were Swein and you'd come up against a seemingly impregnable London, what would you do?"

I thought for a moment.

"Go and get more fighters?" I offered.

"How would that help?" my lord challenged.

"Perhaps he could surround us and starve us out."

"And while he sits here for so long, other parts of the country could be rebelling, even though the thegns have given him hostages."

My lord Edmund seemed to have an argument for all my puny suggestions.

"What do you think, my lord?"

"If I were Swein, Wulfgar, I'd go west. He's already got the north, East Anglia, Mercia and central Wessex. He doesn't have London and the south east – he's met too much opposition here. The other area he doesn't have is the far west. I'd secure that next and then I could come back here."

I felt a trembling inside and all the joy of the Danes' departure seeped from me. I knew he was right.

The high spirits in the royal household continued for another couple of days until news came that sent the mood spiralling down again.

The first piece of news was not unexpected, at least to my lord Edmund. It was as he thought, Swein was now heading west rather than returning up north to lick his few scratches – they could hardly be called wounds.

The second piece of news caused the Queen to declare she was leaving the country and going back to her home in Normandy.

"You can't guarantee this place is safe," she declared to the King. "I'm going to seek the protection of my brother Richard. I've commanded the Abbot of Peterborough to accompany me."

"It'll be a disaster if the Danes capture you," her husband responded. "You'd be a prize hostage."

"If I stay here, I'll be no better off," she scoffed. "I'm going."

"What about the children?" he asked. "They would be valuable hostages too, if caught."

She considered for a moment.

"I'll go alone. If I make it to Normandy, I'll send back for the children."

Rumours she was preparing to flee soon began to circulate around the city. At least the King had not yet decided to abandon the country.

"What was the news that caused my lady the Queen to decide to leave London?" I asked. "Has the whole of the country submitted to Swein?"

My lord Edmund was resting in the shade after a wrestling match with his big brother. I guessed both were trying to keep fit during this period of enforced inactivity. He wiped the beads of sweat from his forehead with the back of his hand.

"There is no news of a total submission, not yet," he

replied, "though it can't be far away. Swein has gone through Wallingford, which he already held, and is heading for Bath, I guess." He sighed. "My stepmother is probably right that we won't be safe for much longer. But what's really worried her is news from the north."

"From the north?"

"Swein left his son Cnut to hold the north and he seems to be achieving that – easily. So easily that he's got married."

"Really?" I hadn't expected him to say that.

"Cnut's young. I don't know ... twenty maybe, perhaps less," my lord continued. "He's made an alliance."

"So it's not a Danish woman he's married."

"No, she's English, a thegn's daughter."

Now I was beginning to understand the significance of the news.

"Someone important?" I asked.

"In northern terms, yes. She's known as Aelfgifu of Northampton, but she is the daughter of Aelfhelm, the late ealdorman of Northumbria."

I frowned, thinking I should know the name.

"He was murdered a few years ago. My father regarded him as a traitor and had his sons blinded. This is their sister; she represents the family now. Cnut's aligning himself with a whole group of discontented men in the north. He's obviously got no plans to go home to Denmark soon, if ever."

By ordering earl Aelfhelm's death, the King had alienated a powerful section of northern society. These people were linked through marriage and other ties. I then remembered my lord had said earl Morcar's wife was a member of this family. Clearly, Morcar must be deep in the Danish camp and that meant Siferth too. What did they feel for King Aethelred? Hatred? Contempt? It was difficult to say. They certainly would have no sense of loyalty to him, for I got the impression earl Aelfhelm was regarded as a victim of court intrigue rather than a true traitor. I was learning fast that to be a thegn could be risky. If the King saw you as a traitor, he'd have you killed and seize your property. There was no weregild, no payment to a bereaved family, if a man had committed such a crime.

There was now a chill in the air, caused partly by the shortening days of autumn and partly by the lack of hope. The Queen had gone. How much longer would the rest of the royal household stay in London?

News came that Swein was at Bath, just as my lord had predicted. It sounded as though the town had capitulated without too much of a fight and Swein seemed to be resting his troops there after their journey west. Several days passed before it became clearer what was going on.

The royal meal was interrupted by a messenger with news.

"I bring news from Bath, my lord," the man declared,

kneeling before the King, who had leaned forward as soon as the traveller hurried into the hall.

"The town has submitted," the King responded. "We've heard that."

"This is to do with earl Aethelmaer," the man added.

"Aethelmaer? He withdrew to a monastery nearly ten years ago!"

"He has come out of the monastery, gathered the western thegns and submitted to the Danes."

I didn't understand the significance of this piece of news, but I did grasp that London and the south-east were now all that was left to the King and there was no way Kent and Sussex could be defended, which meant London was isolated.

There were huddled conversations in corners, people whispering their thoughts, wary glances over the shoulder and gloom everywhere. A meeting of the Witan was called so that the King could consult all his counsellors.

"My stepmother has sent word she has reached Normandy safely," my lord told me. "She saw no Danish boats and so has commanded the Bishop of London to take her children to her."

"Will the King follow?" I asked under my breath.

"We'll see what comes out of the meeting of the Witan," was all he would say.

Would we all be going into exile in Normandy? I wondered. My lord Edmund was exactly that – my lord – and now he was also my family, my life being intertwined with his. But perhaps he didn't see it that way. He was under an obligation to look after me in return for my services, but that didn't necessarily mean he would take me with him wherever he went.

I was distracted by such thoughts, when I felt a firm hand grab my shoulder.

"You're doing nothing," a gruff voice declared and I was pulled round to face its owner.

"My lord?"

I was looking up into the stern visage of the earl of Mercia.

"We need a message taking to Thorkell."

"My lord?"

"He's down at Greenwich. Tell him the King wants him – urgently." He released his grip. "Run!"

I sped off, not because the message was urgent, but because I didn't want to get on the wrong side of Eadric the Greedy. He looked like a man who might turn me into a snack!

I knew my way to Greenwich, but I was wondering how to find this famous Dane. Perhaps someone would know. Down on the riverside I found three ships, unlike anything I'd ever seen before. These were long and sleek, and each end reared up to present a carved head of some fearsome beast. I guessed they must be Danish, so I started asking around. The response from the men on the boats was unintelligible – of course, I realised, they were Danes and spoke their own language. I took to saying simply "Thorkell?" That brought some shouting across the boats and then some pointing to a building near the quay. As I approached it, a man emerged – very blond, but short and stocky.

Is this Thorkell the Tall? I thought. Is he really very short and his name is a joke?

Then I remembered my lord Edmund had said he was truly tall.

"I have a message for Thorkell," I said, wondering how much this little barrel understood.

He signalled me to follow him inside. At first I couldn't see a thing, then my eyes adjusted to the gloom, while my nose took in the pungent smell of fish. There was an exchange of Danish and then the barrel said in English, "What is your message?"

"It is for Thorkell," I replied.

I wanted to see this man for myself and, anyway, a proper messenger always delivers to the right person. These were foreigners, probably Danes, but I couldn't be sure.

A curtain twitched in the corner and was then pulled aside. An incredibly tall man stepped into the room. He had long blond hair, a weather-beaten face and pale blue eyes. His tunic had a great belt round it and into this he stuck his thumbs. He faced me like a giant.

"You are Thorkell?" My voice was little more than a whisper.

He nodded.

"I have a message from the King." I was feeling a little bolder now and I hoped my voice showed that. "The King ... the King has sent me."

Should I order him to the court? The earl had not been particularly polite. I suppose the Dane was in the pay of the English and therefore at their beck and call.

"The King would very much like you to attend on him." I tried to sound gracious rather than imperious. "As soon as possible," I added, as an afterthought.

The barrel said something in Danish and Thorkell listened. Was my translator being more blunt than I had tried to be? I couldn't tell. Thorkell spoke though I understood none of it and the barrel said I could go and tell the King he would come very soon. The blue eyes bore into me. He had got the message. He nodded at me, I gave a little bow and backed out into the street, glad of the fresh air, though secretly delighted I had at last met this famous warlord.

I hurried back with his response.

"Haven't you brought him with you?" was the earl's angry reaction.

"He's coming very soon," I panted, and got out of his way, fast.

Obviously some very important discussions were going on. What great men there were in London – and there weren't that many, as a high number had been in their own areas and had now submitted to the enemy – those left were in consultation with the King as to how to proceed. Unless we could assemble a great army (and that didn't seem very likely), we would be forced to hand London over to the Danes. If we let them besiege us, there was still no hope of victory, for eventually our supplies would run out. We had Thorkell, his ships and some of our own moored slightly downriver, but Swein was hardly likely to try fighting us at sea. It all seemed so hopeless, I felt.

That evening, my lord took me on one side.

"The latest news we have," he told me, "is that Swein appears to be returning up north."

"Oh, is that good?" I asked.

"It's only a temporary respite. He'll be back to claim London, now he has the rest of the country. My father is staying for the time being, as is Thorkell, until it looks as though he has no option but to flee."

I wasn't surprised, but I was sad – our country conquered by Danes.

"But my brothers and I are getting out now."

"And going to Normandy?"

"No, we aren't! We're staying in England, but we'll have to go into hiding."

I could feel my heart beginning to race. Here was an adventure! Hiding from the Danes, spying on them perhaps, working out a way to get rid of them.

"Obviously we'll have to break up our households," my lord continued. "I cannot be somewhere with all my retainers, for that will create suspicion. I shall scatter

35

them between several of my holdings. We have no idea how long this 'exile' will be, for it is like being in exile, cut off from all that is familiar."

So, not an adventure for him, who had known only comfort and privilege in his life.

"And where will I go?" I asked.

"Wulfgar, you're going to become a monk."

CHAPTER 4

We left London the next day. My lord Edmund had sent some of his household west to a holding he had in Wessex, but he took me and half a dozen others with him to go north into Mercia. Our party included a priest called Ealdwine, who had acted as my lord's chaplain for several years. We were being kept in the dark as to our destination, for, if something happened, it was better we knew nothing. Then, even if we were tortured, we couldn't say where the King's son was – if he had escaped. And that was our prime duty – to protect the aetheling at all costs, even if we died doing it.

The journey was quiet and sober. I had my own horse to ride, but knew that once we'd reached our destination I would be back to walking. Only rich people ride horses and so we would have to abandon them in due course.

The mood was sombre and no one wanted to talk of how we were passing through a land controlled by foreigners. Not that we saw any, but we noticed evidence of their presence. In the area around Oxford we saw many homesteads which had been burned to the ground. No doubt, the Danish army had ransacked the barns before setting the thatch alight. The villagers were nowhere to be seen.

Beyond Oxford, we turned west and on the other side of a range of hills, we came to a homestead where we were welcomed and could sleep safely – and in the warm, for our journey had been through the clingy mists of early November.

I found we were guests of earl Leofwine, whose area was the tribeland of the Hwicce. He had short grey hair and beard and soft grey eyes too. I thought he had a kind face, but he looked weary and old.

"The northern lords submitted without a fight," he told us as we ate in his small hall, the fire in the central hearth filling the space with warmth and smoke. "It almost looks like they'd done a deal with Swein before he ever appeared with his fleet, but they've still had to give him hostages, so can't go back now on their invitation, if that's what it was."

"You raised the fyrd round here though?" my lord asked.

"Oh, yes, but our attempts at stopping his progress were pathetic," the earl replied. "You've probably seen what the Danes do to people who get in their way. Fear meant the fighting didn't last long. And ..."

The earl seemed reluctant to continue.

"I think you want to say that some think they will be ruled better by Swein than by my father."

The earl sighed.

"Your father has not always governed justly," he conceded. "There are many grievances. Though whether Swein will prove to be a more just king is anyone's guess. I doubt it personally."

"You didn't have much option but to submit?"

"No, especially with the earl of Mercia not here but in London. I could raise some troops, but not enough."

He gazed into the fire.

"And now we are committed to this Danish ruler," he said with great sadness. "He has my grandson."

"As a hostage?"

"Yes. That's how Swein means to keep us in submission. We dare not misbehave or our kin will suffer. He has hostages from all the leading lords. He holds my grandson, Aethelwine. God help him! I don't see how we are ever going to get our country back."

"My brother Athelstan is particularly friendly with those in the north, indeed I am too, so I'm puzzled by their behaviour. Could they really have *wanted* Swein?"

"I know what you mean. It's likely they would have been very happy with your brother as king, but how was that going to happen? Your father is a good age, but still has his health, so it could be several years before he dies – and I feel certain no one would hurry his death, least of all his own son."

"Impatience then," concluded my lord. "They'd had enough of my father's unjust decisions and couldn't wait any longer, so have taken their chance with Swein. You're right about Athelstan – he'd never do anything to try and take over the kingdom."

"He hasn't married yet?"

"I think he's waiting," my lord answered. "We all know the succession is never sure. If my father dies in, say, the next three years, and he's still king when he dies, then the Witan will choose Athelstan. He's the obvious candidate, for Edward is too young. If my brother had the throne, he would then consider what alliance to make."

"But might the Witan choose you?"

It was a bold question and my lord took some time to answer.

"Athelstan has always been the preferred one," he said at length. "Though he's not as likely to grasp the nettle as I am. But then, perhaps I'm too impulsive." He flashed a smile at his host. "If a pretty girl comes my way, I may grab her!" He leaned back and paused. "Athelstan is more careful, more ... diplomatic. He'd probably make a better king. And anyway, he's my big brother and we're good friends. I'd back him any day."

The next morning we were on the move again, but I noticed that my lord had shed his armour.

"Where's your sword, my lord?" I asked him.

"Earl Leofwine's keeping it for me," he explained. "I'm no longer an aetheling, but simply a poor man who's lost his home and is seeking a new life."

We only did a couple of miles on horseback and then pulled off into a wooded area, where my lord and I dismounted.

"Ealdwine, Wulfgar and I will come with you," he ordered. "The rest of you know where you're heading."

"My lord, I cannot ride while you walk," Ealdwine objected.

"You'll do as I say," was my lord's response. "I remain your lord even though I look like a nobody. And no one must call me 'lord' from now on. Many would sell me to the Danes for a good price."

"No, my ... No, I'm sure they love you too well," Ealdwine countered.

"If a man has no food for his family and himself, he will sell even an aetheling. Now, the rest of you, go! And God go with you!"

We waited until they were well out of sight before we ventured further along the road. It was such a strange feeling – Ealdwine reluctantly riding a horse, my lord proudly walking at his side like a lackey and me trying to keep up.

A few hours brought us to Evesham. At the gates, Ealdwine took the lead, explained our mission and showed we had no weapons. I was wearing my usual tunic, leggings and cloak, but I realised my lord had abandoned his warm woollen cloak for a feeble, thin thing. He was also wearing an old tunic. He certainly didn't look like an aetheling.

We went with Ealdwine to the abbey where he asked to see the abbot. We were shown by the porter into a room near the gatehouse, where we did not wait long before two monks appeared. Ealdwine looked at them intently.

"My business is with the abbot himself," he declared.

"You can speak with me," one of the monks responded.

"No." Ealdwine was firm. "I must speak with Abbot Aelfric and with him alone. Tell him, please, Ealdwine seeks an audience."

The monks shifted on their feet and dithered, giving each other uneasy glances.

"Very well," the leader muttered, and they disappeared.

A tall man with very little hair, and remarkably sprightly for his age, eventually arrived and clasped Ealdwine to his chest.

"My son! How are you? It is *so* long."

"Ah, you do remember me then?" Ealdwine responded, as he was released from the hug.

"I remember your Latin was never very good," the abbot laughed, and Ealdwine smiled.

The abbot glanced at us and raised his eyebrows.

"Please, let us sit. I see you have brought us guests."

"Abbot Aelfric, we come on a serious mission. This man needs a safe place to hide."

"Ah, sanctuary! And what crime have you committed?"

The abbot gave my lord a look that would have pierced his soul and seen if he was lying.

"My crime," my lord began, "is to be born the son of the King."

"He is the aetheling, Edmund, our King's second

42

son," Ealdwine interposed.

The abbot continued to stare at my lord. I could see his eyes taking in the poor clothing.

"An aetheling in disguise?" he commented.

"These are dangerous times," my lord replied. "There will be a price on my head."

"Where is the King, and the rest of the royal family?"

"My father is still in London, for the moment, but I doubt he'll be there for long. The Queen and her children are in Normandy. My brothers are seeking sanctuary in other religious houses. We thought it best to be in different places."

"And how am I to hide you?"

"By treating me as a man pursuing a vocation to join this house."

"And the boy?"

The abbot looked across at me.

"I want him with me," my lord Edmund responded. "I may need him to seek news for me."

"So you are both prepared to follow our way of life, our discipline?"

"Yes." That was my lord.

"And you, boy?"

"I do my lord's bidding – always," was my dutiful response.

"I am the lord here," the abbot replied. "You will do my bidding." He paused. "But I will bear in mind the needs of the country. What's your name, boy?"

43

"Wulfgar."

"Wulfgar, you will call me Father." He turned back to my lord. "You cannot be called Edmund, that's too dangerous. Perhaps Wulfsige and we could say you are brothers, or rather ... " He frowned. "Rather half-brothers in view of the difference in age and your different looks. That will explain your closeness."

"So you will protect them?" Ealdwine asked.

"I will do what I can," the abbot answered. "Only I will know who you really are and you will have to play your part well." He sighed. "That won't be easy. This is a very different life that we lead, one governed by prayer, worship and manual labour. I know thegns sometimes do come to this life, but much later, when they are old, when they begin to worry about their souls."

He looked at me.

"Can you read and write?" he asked.

"No, Father."

"Then I'll put you to work in the kitchen."

"Father," my lord interrupted, "I want Wulfgar to learn to read and write. He will be more useful to me if he can do that and I know you have teachers here."

The abbot frowned.

"I'm not happy with that," he muttered. "He'll do in the kitchen."

"We have brought you a gift," my lord said smoothly, "alms for your monastery."

A bribe! I thought.

"Ealdwine, you have a bag."

The priest produced a cloth bag which, to my eyes, looked quite heavy – a real temptation. The abbot's eyes were on it and I could almost see his wavering.

"We graciously receive your gift," he said at length. "I'll make sure the boy gets some instruction, but he must also help in the kitchen. Working with our hands as well as with our minds is part of the Benedictine way."

I thought working in the kitchen might be quite good, as the days were cold now and the kitchen would be warm. I wasn't so sure about learning from books, as I'd never seen the need for that, but I couldn't disobey.

What really worried me was my hair. Was I going to have the top shaved off leaving me with just an outer fringe, like a proper monk? I was very relieved when the abbot explained we were there 'pursuing a vocation', in other words seeing if it was the right sort of life for us. We would wear the monk's habit, but wouldn't make any vows – yet – and certainly wouldn't have our hair cut. I think my lord Edmund was pleased about that too, though, of course, his main objective was to stay hidden from the Danes and if the cost of that included a hair shave, then so be it.

Ealdwine left us in Evesham as he had simply been there to ensure the abbot accepted us. We had to learn to settle into the monastic rhythm of life – and hide our true identity. To achieve the latter purpose, we agreed to say our common father was Wulfric and we looked like our mothers, who were different wives. We also agreed to say we'd had a terrible experience and were seeking peace and solace to achieve some sort of healing and we didn't want to talk about the past.

The monks in the kitchen did ask me a few questions, but soon let me be and were more concerned that I did what I was told and didn't spoil the cooking.

My lord was elsewhere in the monastery. We shared the dormitory with all the other monks; I was used to sleeping in odd places and in the cold, but I think my lord found it hard. We had to get up at midnight for Matins and later in the night for the office of Lauds, then back to bed for a couple of hours before getting up properly for Prime. There were eight services altogether, every three hours – as the abbot had warned us, there was a great deal of prayer and worship.

Except for getting up in the night, it was a fairly pleasant life. I enjoyed helping to prepare the food and as I had thought, the kitchen was a warm place to be. I wasn't so enamoured with learning my letters, as the scriptorium was cold and the teacher was strict. I hoped I wouldn't be there forever, but I'd heard nothing about Swein or the King, and, stuck there in Evesham, we certainly weren't doing anything to recover the country for the English.

So I was very pleased when one night, not long before Christmas, my lord managed to whisper a message to me.

"We're going on a journey tomorrow," he said softly.

"Not far, only to Worcester, but you are to come as well."

That was something to look forward to, although the excitement of a break from the routine and a visit to a new place was tempered by a cold journey on foot.

CHAPTER 5

The ground was hard with a thick white frost and our breath came out as clouds. I was glad of the thick cloak I had been loaned and I pulled it round me in an effort to keep warm.

We were a group of five – three monks, my lord and I. We let the monks do the talking, so I knew we were heading for the monastery in Worcester, but whether our purpose in going was the same as theirs I had no idea. I presumed my lord had some very good reason for walking some fifteen miles on a bitterly cold day.

We reached Worcester just as the light was fading. The monastery there seemed very similar to that at Evesham, so there was no danger of getting lost. The chapel, the refectory and the dormitory were all in the same places as though there was a standard design for a monastery.

After some refreshment, my lord and I were taken to a room where a monk was writing at a table.

"Wulfgar, this is our host," my lord said, kissing the monk's outstretched hand and indicating I should do the same. "He is Wulfstan, the Bishop of Worcester, and also the Archbishop of York."

The Archbishop smiled at us both. His wiry grey hair stuck up, forming a crown on his head and he had deep lines on his face, but his eyes were bright with life. The hand I had kissed was bony with enlarged knuckles and wrinkled skin. I thought he must be very old. He signalled us to sit down.

"I hear you have a new name." He addressed my lord.

"I'm known as Wulfsige and the monks think Wulfgar and I are brothers."

The Archbishop nodded.

"Very wise. No one can be trusted," was his comment. "You seek news, of course."

"I know you travel widely," my lord responded, "and I heard you would be in Worcester for Christmas."

"Indeed, and what I see breaks my heart."

The Archbishop moved the paper he had been writing and leaned his arm on his table. He slowly shook his head.

"There is so much suffering." He sighed. "But then, we are not a nation that honours God, so what else can we expect?"

My lord was silent and I wondered what he was thinking.

"There is so little loyalty these days," the Archbishop continued, "and people do not stand up for what is right."

"Are you thinking of Swein's conquest?" asked my lord.

"Partly. There was very little resistance." He paused. "Men are brave when the enemy is not there – full of words as to how they will fight. But when face to face with him, they crumple. I've heard of a thegn who allowed the Danes to defile his wife. Ten of them had her, one after the other and he simply stood by."

"Oh, God have mercy!"

My lord had gone pale and I suddenly thought of the pretty lady Frida and wondered if earl Siferth would have fought to keep her honour.

"Also slaves are escaping from their thegns and joining the Danes," the Archbishop told us. "And you know what that means? In a fight between the English and the Danes, if a slave kills his former master, no weregild is paid, but if the thegn kills his former slave, the Danes ensure weregild is paid – and at the rate of a thegn, for the slave is a freeman in their society. You see there is little justice left in the world, but this is what we have earned, for we have not followed the way of Christ and lived according to his laws."

My lord was quiet, perhaps thinking about some of his father's poor decisions.

"I have never forgotten," he responded eventually, "though it is more than ten years ago now, how my father ordered the killing of the Danes on St. Brice's Day. I cannot think that was right."

"It was indeed a wicked act and I believe some of our present troubles stem from it," the Archbishop agreed. "But there are other things. Widows are wrongfully forced into marriage and too many are reduced to poverty and greatly humiliated. And the poor are trodden down, often defrauded and sold as slaves to serve in a foreign land. Did you know," he said, staring at me, "that if a man steals with the knowledge of his family, then all are liable to penal slavery?"

I stared back and shook my head.

"Even the child in the cradle!" he exclaimed. "It's in our laws, but it is wrong. No child should be enslaved because its parent has stolen, and probably stolen to provide food to the starving. God is angry and we are being punished."

"But even if the Danes have been sent to us as God's instrument of punishment, surely we shouldn't just let them conquer us?" my lord countered.

"Though they are not all pagans, they do not honour God in their cruelty," the Archbishop acknowledged. "And you, as a leader in our land, have a responsibility to protect your people."

I was bursting to ask a question, but wasn't sure I should. He caught my eye though and I suddenly felt brave.

"The scripture says something about being hit on the cheek and not hitting back," I blurted out.

"Ah! This boy has been listening to the words of Christ," he commented. "That is an important saying of our Lord, but sometimes misunderstood. Christ said if we are hit on the right cheek, we should offer our left cheek to our attacker. Yes?"

I nodded as I remembered I'd heard that.

"For a man to hit you on the right cheek, how does he use his hand, assuming he's using his right hand?"

I thought for a moment.

"He must use the back of his hand," I answered.

"That is how a man hits his slave," he commented. "And to hit you on the left cheek, how will he do it?"

"He will have to use the palm of his hand."

"And that is to hit you as an equal and not as his inferior. By offering your left cheek, you shame your opponent and he should desist. The scripture is not saying we should not resist evil," the Archbishop concluded.

"I don't have a problem with fighting back," my lord informed him. "But there is somewhere in scripture where God says he'll do the fighting for us and we don't have to do it. That puzzles me."

"You may be thinking of Moses," the Archbishop replied. "Faced with an Egyptian army on his heels and an impassable stretch of water before him, what could he do to save himself and the Israelites? Not a lot. God told him to trust and then he parted the waters." He was lost in thought momentarily. "You need wisdom, my son, to know how to fight and how to return this country to the ways of God. In the meantime, what did Christ say? We are to pray for our enemies."

"I want to pray Swein and Cnut die and the Danes give up and go home!" my lord declared.

"I do not think it right to pray that a man's end is hastened," the Archbishop countered. "St. Paul talks of heaping live coals on the heads of our enemies."

"Oh, that'll do! They'll soon leave us alone if that happens."

"No, that is not a hostile gesture," responded the cleric. "St. Paul says if our enemy is hungry we are to feed him; if he is thirsty we are to give him drink for by so doing we heap burning coals on his head. By showing him love, not vengeance, we shame him, we make him burn with shame."

"I can't see that," my lord objected. "If we feed the Danes or help them in any way, they'll simply take it as a sign of weakness and oppress us even more."

"I agree it sounds like an unreal ideal," the Archbishop acknowledged. "God's ways are not often our ways. In the present circumstances, the most needful thing for this nation is that we repent. There must be a return to justice and loyalty. I have already been committing some of these thoughts to paper. I have written this:

Now too often a kinsman does not protect a kinsman any more than a stranger, neither a father his son, nor sometimes a son his own father, nor one brother another, nor has anyone of us ordered his life as he should, neither ecclesiastics according to rule nor laymen according to law. But we have made desire a law unto us all too often, and have kept neither the precepts nor laws of God or man as we should. Nor has anyone had loyal intentions towards another as justly as he should, but almost everyone has deceived and injured another by word or deed; and in particular almost everyone wrongly stabs another in the back with shameful attack.

Sadly, your father's reign began with great treachery – the death of Edward, the lawful king. And though your father took no part in that, he has innocent blood on his hands. And has added to that in his own right and of his own volition. There is corruption and sin, betrayal and fraud, as well as men not being true to their marriage vows."

I thought my lord appeared to blush at that.

"You are right to reprove my father," he admitted. "He has defiled the marriage bed and there are men who have suffered through his injustice." He sighed. "Our nation is indeed being sorely punished. So what can we do?" he begged.

"Lead a blameless life yourself, care for those in your charge, pray God's blessing on your enemies and hold no hatred in your heart for them," was the Archbishop's advice. "This is not an easy path, but the Spirit of God is with you to help you and to give you wisdom."

After our meeting, I felt I'd heard several sermons all in one service! But I was impressed. This man spoke powerfully and persuasively. Indeed, my lord urged him to put more of his thoughts on paper and then distribute them to the church throughout the land.

We didn't stay long in Worcester and were soon back in Evesham. Christmas was very close now, but the period before that was a time of soul-searching, penitence and preparation. We had it impressed upon us that not only were we about to celebrate Christ's incarnation, his first coming into the world – that as a human being – but that we were anticipating his return, as the all-conquering God. I imagined Jesus sweeping through our land like Swein. The monks said he would come as judge, so perhaps it would even be as bad as Swein, with people being punished for their wrongdoing. I hadn't really thought about the Christ coming back and it was a bit scary.

"You'll be alright," one monk told me, "as long as you are loyal to God and not flirting with the enemy."

He'd winked at me, as though 'flirting with the enemy' had significance. The only flirting I ever saw was between girls twice my age and men even older.

Christmas itself was something of a disappointment. There was plenty of joy in the services (which went on even longer than usual), but the food was still fairly basic. At court there would have been wild boar and amazing sweet treats and everyone would have been vying to tell the best riddle, but in the monastery the feasting was far more sober. I decided I didn't want to be a monk and every time I went to chapel I prayed God would send the Danes back home. I left it up to him as to how that could be done.

The Archbishop had been able to give us very little definite news. He reported that Swein had indeed gone back north and he expected him to spend Christmas at

Gainsborough. But he had no news of London or of the King.

The day before the Feast of the Epiphany, I was sent for by the abbot. I couldn't think of anything I had done wrong and I was even doing quite well with my letters, but there were so many little things that I could have messed up unintentionally. I knocked warily on his door and went in when he called. My lord was already in there.

"Wulfgar, come in and sit down," the abbot said. "We have been talking and have decided you are needed for a mission."

CHAPTER 6

The snow came that night as we celebrated the coming of the wise men to see the child Jesus.

"Would they have travelled through snow?" I asked my teacher.

"No, they came from a hot country and there isn't any snow in the land of the Jews," he answered. "Anyway, we don't know when the Christ was born – it may not have been winter. Also, it took the Magi many months to make the journey and the Christ-child was no longer in the stable, but in a house."

Great flakes floated to the ground and I wondered about the journey I was to make and whether it would be postponed, but it wasn't.

The day we set out (four monks and me) the sun was creeping up over the hills and casting long shadows over the deep snow. The trackways were beaten down by the feet of men and the hooves of animals, so as long as we followed a main route, we shouldn't find our journey too difficult. We were bound for Winchcombe, about ten miles away.

I was really cold and tired when we got there and I couldn't stop shivering. The guestmaster, Brother Brihthelm, took me under his wing and gave me some hot broth.

"Whatever made them send you here in this weather?" he muttered.

I pretended I didn't need to reply and simply thanked him for his kindness.

In the early evening service I had my first opportunity to look around at the monks. I sought a familiar face and, when I found it, I kept my eyes on it until its owner saw he was watched and blinked in recognition. When the service ended, we both lingered. I pulled back into the shadows and let others leave, while he went to kneel before a statue of Christ. Once we were alone, I joined him, kneeling as though in prayer.

"Wulfgar," he whispered. "Is all well?"

"Yes. He's sent me for news. We've seen Archbishop Wulfstan, but he doesn't know much."

"I have more. Tell my brother that London has submitted and my ... the King with Thorkell has spent Christmas on the Isle of Wight. By now, he has probably fled to Normandy." Lord Athelstan paused. "That's all I know."

"I'll tell him. I don't think he'll be surprised."

I left him praying, though what he prayed for I don't know. He was an aetheling without much hope of ever gaining a throne and had apparently been betrayed by men who claimed to be his friends.

As I left the chapel a monk stepped from the gloom and grabbed my arm. I recognised Brother Brihthelm.

"What are you here for?" he demanded. "You stopped to speak to Ordwulf."

"Ordwulf? I don't know anybody called Ordwulf." I

was having to think fast. "Oh, is that the name of that man who's praying? I simply wanted to thank the Lord for a safe journey."

He was staring at me. I had to keep my head, so I opened my eyes wide and stared back at him, desperately praying he would think I was telling the truth. He released my arm, frowned slightly and muttered, "Well, I'm glad you've stopped shivering now. But I'm not sure I believe you, so I'm taking you to the abbot."

I was dragged off to face the head of the monastery. It was good for me that the abbot dismissed Brother Brihthelm and interviewed me alone.

"Brother Brihthelm believes you were talking to our guest, Ordwulf," he accused, his eyes fixed on my face.

I returned his gaze, but said nothing.

"My fellow monks suspect he may be a criminal who's seeking sanctuary. However, I know Ordwulf has two brothers," he continued after a pause, "and I would not be surprised if you have come from one of them."

He raised his eyebrows by way of query and I wondered what I should say.

"Do you come from Edmund or Eadwig?"

It looked as though the abbot knew *everything*.

"My lord Edmund," I admitted.

He smiled.

"Your secret is safe. What news did you bring?"

I told him and, after a short conversation, he let me go, assuring me he would say nothing.

Outside his door, I let my heartbeat go back to normal before I went looking for the refectory.

My lord Athelstan and I did not acknowledge each other again in case we caused men to suspect us. Of course, he didn't know we'd been watched as we pretended to pray, but Brother Brihthelm didn't challenge me again. After a couple of days, I returned with the others to Evesham. The snow had begun to melt and we had a muddy journey back north.

My lord was pleased his brother was safe and well, but he was greatly saddened by the news.

"London submitted? I suppose they had no choice once the court had left and Thorkell too. What other option did they have? Now Swein has the whole country."

"Not the Isle of Wight," I prompted.

"That'll not be for long. My father has lost his kingdom."

Any joy of Christmas had gone and a heaviness settled on him, about which I could do very little.

I had hardly settled into the usual routine again when I found myself once more summoned to see the abbot.

"We have another mission for you, Wulfgar," my lord told me and he almost smiled. "Archbishop Wulfstan is going to York and has suggested you join his party. You can move among people without being noticed and bring me word on the mood of the city."

"These are difficult times," the abbot stated. "The Archbishop can travel freely for Swein does not want to interrupt the work of the church. It would not be safe for your lord to go as someone might recognise him."

I couldn't think of anything to say! I was going to York, it was as simple as that and I was to act as eyes and ears for my lord. When I thought about it, I felt sure it would be good. At least I could get out and about, whereas my lord was like a wild boar which had been caged and which fretted to be free.

It was mid January when I set off from Worcester with the Archbishop's party. I had no idea how far York was – all I knew was that it was in the far north, further than I had ever been in my life. I was very glad I didn't have to walk! I soon realised the Archbishop must be very rich, for all of us had horses, even me, and as well as monks there were lay brothers in our party who acted as servants.

No one seemed to question my presence. I reckoned some of them didn't even notice me and I decided that my best course of action was to stay quiet and out of the way.

As on the journey from London to Evesham, I noticed some settlements we passed through had been destroyed. Wherever we came to a church that was still standing (for even some of the churches had been burned by the Danes), we would stop and the Archbishop would pray there.

Once we crossed Watling Street, we saw no signs of destruction and there were people still living in all the villages. Sometimes we received hospitality from a monastery and sometimes from a thegn or leading man in an area. We were well fed! We were now in the greater season of Christmas, so still a time of feasting. That would end at Candlemas and within weeks we would be passing into Lent with all its fasting. I wasn't looking forward to that – the period before Christmas had been bad enough and Lent was nearly twice the length. But, in the depth of January, Lent seemed a long way off and I had a mission to accomplish.

I was amazed by York. There seemed to be water everywhere – well, the snow had melted and the winter rains had also helped to raise the water level in the river. The town was surrounded by water and the air was damp and chill. That dampness got into me and I struggled ever to be warm.

The streets (they called them 'gates') were narrow and very busy with people pushing carts and not caring who they hit with them and shouting abuse. The language was so strange too; then I realised York had been under Viking control for, perhaps, a hundred years and some people spoke Norse, while some spoke English, and others spoke a mixture.

When I sat round a fire with the locals, I found all they talked about were their women and their trade. They boasted of their conquests (not all the women had been willing) and of the money they were making. I never heard anyone mention Swein or Cnut or even the Danes. I guessed these people didn't care much, as long as they were left in peace and as long as York was able to trade unhindered by pirates.

One evening, the Archbishop had a visit from a man who was blind and who was guided everywhere by a boy about my age. I was sitting in the shadows, but the visitor had no idea I was there anyway.

"You are well, my son?" the Archbishop asked.

"I keep in good health," the visitor replied, "and I am grateful that I have those who act as my eyes."

"What is life like under a new ruler?" was the next question.

"Swein treats us well," he answered. "We have no complaint. York is not beset by hostile ships, so trade is good. He has control now of the whole of the east coast and nothing stops our trade across the northern sea."

"And your sister?"

"She is with child, so Cnut may soon have an heir."

"Swein means to stay in England?"

"His son Harald rules Denmark for him and rules it well, so he has no need to return until England is fully subjugated. And that can't be far off, for Aethelred is fled to Normandy. Good riddance!"

"You know you should forgive him," the Archbishop chided.

"Forgive! Huh. He listened to the poison dripped into him by that weasel from Mercia. There wasn't even an attempt at a trial. My father was the guest – some guest! – of Eadric in Shrewsbury and on a hunting trip he happened to be killed." His voice was harsh. "Of course, that was not all. The King then ordered us to be blinded. We could easily have died ourselves. So we are mutilated and dishonoured. And I should forgive him?"

I shivered, but not from cold. This was why they had welcomed Swein and seen him as a man who would give them justice in an unfair kingdom.

When his visitor had gone, Archbishop Wulfstan called me to his side.

"I suppose you heard all that," he said.

I nodded.

"Do you know who that man is?"

"One of the sons of the late earl Aelfhelm of Northumbria," I replied.

"Oh!" He raised his wiry eyebrows. "You are well versed. You know he was blinded on the orders of the King."

"Yes, and his sister is now married to Cnut."

"And expecting his child," the Archbishop added. "That man was Ufegeat. Your lord will have met both him and his brother Wulfheah. As you heard, he does not speak well of Aethelred. There's no love lost there. It is understandable, but sad. Unless he does forgive, the bitterness will eat away at his heart."

I was quiet, but I was thinking that if I'd been in Ufegeat's shoes I'd have been as bitter as him.

"Betrayal is a terrible thing," the Archbishop was talking almost to himself. "A man is your guest, but you have invited him so that he can die – that is great treachery. If earl Aelfhelm was guilty of some crime, then let him be tried and if he is to die, then he can at least prepare to meet his Maker, he can be shrived. But there was no possibility of preparation. Who knows where his soul is now?"

I wasn't expected to answer!

"And there is no shame, no regret," he continued. "I have often been with the King and with the earl of Mercia and they have always sought to justify their actions. Good deeds are reviled and bad deeds are praised. We need to repent sincerely for what we have done wrong."

He looked at me, as though suddenly aware of my presence.

"Keep praying, Wulfgar, keep praying!" he urged. "That is our only hope."

I wasn't sure we prayed for the same things, but both of us would shortly be stunned by news and wonder what part our prayers had had in bringing it about.

CHAPTER 7

On the eve of Candlemas the Archbishop called me to his side.

"Wulfgar, I have been considering your return to Evesham."

I looked at his harried face, but said nothing.

"I shall not be leaving York just yet, as I have to consecrate a new bishop for London. You know what happened to the last one?"

"Was he battered to death with ox bones?"

He gave a rare smile.

"That was Aelfheah the saintly Archbishop of Canterbury," he explained. "His replacement, Lyfing, I trust is still alive, but cannot act as archbishop until he has been to Rome and received his pallium from the Pope. No. I hope the previous bishop of London is also still alive. He took the Queen's children into exile – and stayed."

"So Swein is allowing you to make a new one to replace him?"

He laughed.

"I don't need Swein's permission," he responded. "My king is Christ, so I *consecrate* men to be bishops even if the Danes then do not allow them to act as such. But, so far, Swein has seen no need to oppose the work of the church. After all, we help to keep the people quiet. Scripture says, 'Obey those in authority'."

"Even usurpers?"

"Hush, Wulfgar. Swein is king of England now, all have submitted. You could get your tongue cut out for such talk."

He fiddled with the cross that hung round his neck.

"You came to collect news for your lord," he said at length, "and you do have news to take."

"None that will encourage him," I declared.

The Archbishop nodded.

"I know, but at least he will see how strong the support for Swein is up here. It will be far less in the south."

He paused.

"I think that it would be good for you to return soon. You should certainly be back in Evesham well before Lent which begins on the 10th of March. I shall arrange an escort, for I need to send messages anyway and you can travel with my men at least as far as Worcester."

I wasn't expected to comment, as I had no option in the matter. In fact, I was happy to be returning to my lord, for I found York akin to a foreign land.

I had celebrated Candlemas before, but never in such an important place and in such an important church. York had been Christian for a long time – it was the Canterbury of the north – and its church was impressive. Like many churches it had a long, thin nave and a high ceiling, with small windows set high up and which threw light on to the floor. But it also had a large area at the end beyond a stone screen for the Archbishop, the priests and the monks who sang there every day. Seeing it filled with candles that evening was awe-inspiring.

The account of the visit by the Blessed Virgin Mary and Joseph to the Temple with the baby Jesus was read and the Archbishop in his sermon pounced on the phrase 'a sword shall pierce thy heart'. He said that while this was a prophecy to the Virgin of how she would see her Son suffer, it was also a word to us.

"A sword has pierced many hearts in our land," he preached. "Some of you grieve the loss of loved ones, but more than that, our nation has suffered losses and insults. Do we feel shame? All the insults that we often suffer we repay with honouring those who insult us. We pay them continually."

I wondered if he was talking about the money the King had given in the past to buy off Danish aggression.

"They humiliate us daily; they ravage and they burn, plunder, rob and carry on board," he continued.

Well, I thought, Swein won't like this if he hears of it.

"Lo, what else is there in all these events except God's anger, clear and visible over this people?"

Oh, he's saying it's our fault the Danes are our masters.

"It is no wonder that things go wrong for us, for we know full well that now for many years men have too often not cared what they did by word or deed, but this people has become very corrupt through manifold sins and many misdeeds."

He carried on berating us about betrayal, theft, murder, adultery and the selling of people to foreigners. Then he turned to attacks on the church.

"There are fierce persecutors of the church and cruel tyrants, all too many, and widespread scorn of divine laws and Christian virtues. Too often good deeds are reviled with derision and God-fearing people are blamed all too greatly and especially are those reproached and all too often treated with contempt who love right and possess the fear of God in any extent."

The answer, he proclaimed, was to repent.

"Intercede eagerly with God himself," he urged. "Let us turn to what is right and leave wrongdoing, and atone very zealously for what we have done amiss."

He wasn't pulling any punches and the sermon certainly did nothing to cheer me, but then, I supposed, perhaps we needed to hear that we'd done wrong and how our present troubles were the result. If we repented, would Swein go away? I couldn't see that happening, for he knew he'd conquered a rich and fertile land.

Later, as I lit a candle, I prayed that the Almighty God would give us some light in the gloom, some sign of hope, something I could tell my lord that would lift his spirits and give him a reason to go on fighting with his brother for our country.

At the end of the service, the light of Christmas was extinguished and we filed out of the church in the dark.

A couple of days later, I was down by the riverside watching the boats and listening to the raucous chatter of the traders, when a boat came in sight, travelling at speed using both a sail and oarsmen. Everyone stopped to watch it. It berthed near where I stood and there was an immediate shouting of news – in Danish was my guess, as I couldn't understand it.

Whatever the news was, it was causing a great stir, for men were rushing off in all directions. I grabbed someone.

"What's happened?" I asked.

He stared at me and then uttered two words, "Swein dead."

"Dead?!"

But he'd gone, running off down the quay – and I ran too, as fast as I could.

The Archbishop was entertaining some visitors when I stumbled into his presence and he didn't look best pleased by the interruption.

"Wulfgar? What do you mean by this?"

"Swein's dead!" I gasped, and flopped on the floor exhausted.

Everyone else was on their feet in seconds, but I had run so hard I was spent and they had to wait while I got my breath and could tell them about the boat.

I'm not sure what happened next for people began to appear from all parts of the house as the news spread out like a fire. A servant arrived who backed up my tale.

"It's true," he confirmed. "The news is spreading quickly through the town. Swein has died – at Gainsborough."

"Was he killed or what?" asked the Archbishop.

"The word at the moment is that he suddenly became ill, took to his bed and died."

"When?"

"On the 2nd."

Candlemas! Even as we were lighting our candles, down in Gainsborough the Danish leader was sick. I imagined his dying at the very moment we blew out all our candles, but I don't know if that's really how it happened. The stunning truth was that Swein had gone; the fearsome warlord was dead.

And now?

The Archbishop's residence became even busier than usual with numerous visitors. Among those who came was Ufegeat, the blinded son of Aelfhelm.

"Wulfgar, look after Ulf, while my guest and I go and pray."

The Archbishop indicated I was to entertain Ufegeat's young guide. The lad promptly came and sat by me while the two men left the room.

"Pray!" he scoffed. "They just want to talk where they think no one's listening, but I know what they'll say."

"You do?"

"They want to talk about the death of the King."

My heart missed a beat as I wondered if he meant

Aethelred, but I quickly realised he was talking about Swein.

"Everyone's talking about it," Ulf proclaimed, "and wondering what will happen. But I know."

"You do?"

"His son will be king," he stated. "It's obvious."

I didn't think it was obvious, but decided to keep my mouth shut and pretend I was a bit stupid.

"I heard a riddle the other day. Do you want to hear it?" Ulf asked.

"Yes."

"So, what am I describing?

    I am a strange creature for I satisfy women.
    I grow very tall, erect in a bed,
    I'm hairy underneath. From time to time
    A beautiful girl, the brave daughter
    Of some fellow dares to hold me,
    Grips my reddish skin, robs me of my head
    And puts me in the pantry. At once that girl
    With plaited hair who has confined me
    Remembers our meeting. Her eye moistens."

I made my face as blank as I could.

"So what is it? Don't you know?"

I shook my head, pretending I didn't have a clue.

"It's an onion!" he laughed.

"Oh, yes, I suppose it is," I answered.

"But it has another meaning." He winked at me. "Like a lot of our riddles, it's rude."

"Is it?" I was playing my part very well, I thought, for I knew both meanings of the riddle.

"If you tell it in company, men will guffaw and women titter," he boasted.

"I'll remember."

I was actually thinking, how much longer have I got to put up with this cocky lad?

"How long have you been in the Archbishop's household?" Ulf asked.

"Not long."

"Are you going to be a monk?" was the next question.

"I don't know."

"It doesn't matter if you are, you know. They all have women and some are not even discreet about it."

I wasn't going to argue with him, but from what I'd seen, I didn't agree. The monks I'd met seemed to me to be genuinely godly men, concerned to do the will of the Lord and follow the example of Christ. Admittedly, the Archbishop was more a man of the world and clearly involved in politics, but I thought he led a fairly blameless life. He certainly didn't have a secret concubine.

I was very glad when I saw the Archbishop returning with Ufegeat on his arm. Ulf saw them and leaned to whisper in my ear, "Harald will be made king."

I didn't need to feign surprise, for I was astonished by his prediction.

After that encounter, I kept my ears open for news of Swein's son Harald, but I didn't hear him mentioned. The

Archbishop, however, was keeping me away from any interesting conversations. If he had a visitor and I was around, he would send me off on a mission or he would take his visitor into another part of his residence, away from my flapping ears. I could still walk the town and pick up gossip, but I learned no more. All I could establish was that Swein had died naturally, though unexpectedly.

I was itching to go back to my lord. The Archbishop had mentioned it, but then nothing had happened, so I decided to ask him if I could go. Before I had the opportunity, he called me to him.

"Wulfgar, you are to begin your return journey tomorrow. All is arranged and I have some particular news that I wish you to carry to your lord."

CHAPTER 8

We made better progress back to Worcester without the Archbishop and as we travelled we shared the news of Swein, though some places already knew. From there, I set out for Evesham. I wondered if my lord Edmund had already heard and also how long it would take the news to reach London and then Normandy. But would it make any difference to our country? From what the Archbishop had told me, I wasn't sure it would.

My lord was very pleased to see me, and he took me into the abbot's room, so he could hear my news too.

"The rumour is Swein's dead," he declared.

"It's true," I reported. "He died on the Feast of Candlemas."

"But how?" the abbot asked.

"He felt ill and, within hours, he was dead," I told them. "There's no suggestion of foul play."

"May his soul rest in peace," the cleric prayed.

"This is wonderful news!" my lord cried. "Now we have hope. We'll get our land back."

"The Archbishop gave me particular information that ..."

"By your face, it is not good news." My lord was checked in his delight.

"The northern lords have made a decision about who should rule in Swein's place."

"And it is not my father?"

"It is not the King," I confirmed. "They've chosen Cnut."

"They have submitted to that ... whippersnapper?"

"Yes. The Archbishop said I was to make it very clear to you that they don't want the King back, as his rule was so unjust. But ..." I paused.

"But?"

"He thinks Mercia and Wessex may not feel the same," I added. "Though there is a problem."

"Which is?"

"The hostages. Cnut has all the hostages who were given to Swein. Their lives are in danger if the lords do not submit."

He was quiet.

"Some hard choices will have to be made," was the abbot's contribution.

That was an understatement!

The news of Cnut's accession certainly dampened my lord's spirits.

"I must get a message to earl Leofwine," he decided.

He didn't send me. In fact, I seemed to be unwanted now I had brought him the news from York. I returned to the kitchen and my learning, and wondered what was happening. I did hear that earl Leofwine had come to the abbey. I don't know if this was because my lord sent for him or if he came seeking advice after news reached him of Swein's death, for clearly Mercia and Wessex now had to decide whether or not to submit to Cnut.

I did once think about Ulf and his prediction of Harald. That was Swein's eldest son, but it looked as though he would rule Denmark on his own now his father was dead and leave little brother Cnut to fight for his inheritance in England.

I hoped we would fight for it this time. We had let the Danes overrun us with hardly a whimper. Now they had an untried youth at their head – surely we could send him back home?

The matter of the hostages was a worry, but hostages were the norm in any warfare – it was the obvious way to keep the defeated in their place. The English did it as well as foreigners, though on this occasion, Cnut had English hostages but we had no Danes. Sometimes their lives were sacrificed – that was one of the perils of war. The cost of our independence could be the lives of young men like earl Leofwine's grandson.

I was getting frustrated – and I was getting scolded by both the monks in the kitchen and the monk who taught me writing because of my lack of attention. I wanted some action. I was sure something was happening, but I could hardly ask outright. The life of the monastery continued in its usual way.

So I was delighted when my lord told me I was to go with him to Winchcombe. That meant a meeting with lord Athelstan I felt sure, and I hoped I would be allowed to sit in the corner and listen.

An icy wind blew through us as we travelled.

February was about to give way to March, but it wasn't going quietly and we had a raw journey. I remembered I had arrived shivering in Winchcombe once before, and this time our party was treated to hot broth again before the monks disappeared in one direction and we went to the abbot's room.

"Athelstan!" My lord hugged his brother. "You're well?"

"As well as one can be in these days," he answered. "But you look very fit, little brother."

"I've no horse now, so I walk everywhere and I've been exercising too," my lord responded. "I've no intention of staying in a monastery forever."

The abbot coughed and my lord belatedly greeted him.

"I'll leave you to talk," the abbot said. "If you need anything, send your boy."

So I did get to sit in the corner and I hoped they wouldn't need the abbot.

"I've seen earl Leofwine and he thinks Mercia and Wessex may refuse to submit," my lord began.

"The news is even better than that," lord Athelstan replied. "The northern lords have acknowledged Cnut, but the southern lords don't want him. Well, who would? He's very young – an untried warrior compared with his father. Wessex and Mercia want our father back."

"That's wonderful news!"

"But it's conditional."

"Conditional on what?" my lord asked.

"They have told him that no lord is dearer to them than their natural lord and he is invited to return if, note this, if he will govern them more justly than he did before."

There was an intake of breath by my lord.

"They don't want a repeat of harsh taxes and people being punished who didn't pay," lord Athelstan explained. "The King has demanded high rates of heriot from heirs who claim their inheritance – too high the lords say. They also complain he deprived people of their property for too wide a range of misdemeanours."

My lord nodded.

"We know he hasn't ruled wisely," he acknowledged. "There were good men he excluded from his counsel."

"And one man who's been allowed too much power."

I guessed he meant earl Eadric.

"So what is happening now?" my lord asked.

"A delegation has gone to Normandy with those terms. We're waiting for a reply."

"More waiting," complained my lord Edmund. "How I hate this waiting!"

"We must be patient, brother. With the north backing Cnut, it won't be easy for our father to re-establish his rule. Also London is infested with Danes."

"I suppose it must be. And elsewhere?"

"There are no Danes in Mercia and Wessex. Swein didn't have a huge force and he recruited English from the north who fought for him – at a price I believe. But they couldn't be relied on. No, he's kept control through having hostages. If Wessex and Mercia refuse Cnut, all Cnut can do is kill the hostages. But London is fortified by some Danes and I don't think they'll give in to us easily. Think how hard it was for Swein to take the city last year."

"He didn't manage it," my lord agreed. "It only fell to the Danes when it was clear the whole of the rest of England was in his hands." He paused. "So we could have a repeat of last autumn's situation but in reverse, the English trying to get London back."

Both of them were lost in thought for a while.

"What news of Eadwig?" my lord broke the silence.

"He's well. I've sent carefully phrased letters to Ely to keep him informed," lord Athelstan told him. "It's best he stays there for the time being. If there is some fighting, you and I may have to leave these disguises behind, but he's a bit young to take up the sword just yet."

"Earl Leofwine has my sword and armour. I can soon recover it if the call comes."

My lord's spirits were definitely raised by our visit to Winchcombe. I even heard him whistling on the journey home, something the monks frowned on, but my lord was oblivious to their disapproval. If they had their suspicions about our true identity, they said nothing, but I don't think they guessed. After all, why should an aetheling be in a monastery? I reckoned my lord had chosen a good place to hide.

Back in Evesham, we had to resume our life of prayer and work, and exercise patience. Lent was creeping up on us, for Ash Wednesday fell on March the 10th that year and I knew that would usher in a grim, penitential time, the only positive in my view being that the days were getting longer and there might soon be the scent of spring in the air.

Earl Leofwine paid a visit on Shrove Tuesday for I heard about it later that day when my lord took me aside in a quiet corner.

"There's been a meeting," he quietly informed me. "My father sent over Edward and some messengers and they met with the southern lords."

"Edward?"

"My half-brother."

"But he's younger than me!"

"He was well-protected. It's a statement." My lord grunted. "My father is signalling his support for Edward as his heir, even though he's so young. Anyway, he didn't have much to say on his own behalf. He came to deliver my father's reply to the conditional invitation."

I could hardly breathe with wondering what had happened.

"My father sent his greetings to *all* his people. He has promised to be a gracious lord to everyone and to reform all the things they complained about. He says the past should be forgiven and there can be a fresh start as long as – and he's issued his own condition – as long as *everyone* now turns to him without treachery."

"So all the lords who submitted to Swein will now turn back to the King?"

"It sounds as though the ones who submitted last year will be forgiven as long as they return to the fold *now*. If anyone continues to back the Danish claim, they won't get any mercy from my father. Earl Leofwine says those who met Edward gave their oaths and all agreed that every Danish king is an exile from England forever."

"And now the King will come back, as he has the support of the south. What will he do about the north?" I wanted to know.

"He's got to recapture London first, only then can he say he has control of the south and can turn his attention to the north. If the northern lords submit quickly, I think he will show mercy. What we don't know is how strong Cnut is. He's very young, not even twenty, but he may be a man who inspires loyalty. Of course, he too could be making rich promises."

He shook his head and frowned.

"I do hope my father keeps these promises he's made," he muttered. "If he doesn't, we're in serious trouble."

Thus we entered Lent hopeful but unsure, confident the King would return but wondering how he could regain his authority completely. Of course, I was not my lord's close companion, so he only chose to tell me certain things and I suspected that messages were passing between him and his brother that I knew nothing about.

Two weeks passed and then I was summoned to the abbot's room where I saw a familiar face.

"Father Ealdwine!" I greeted the priest with a broad smile.

"You look well, Wulfgar. Does the life of the monastery suit you?"

I looked around. Both the abbot and my lord Edmund were smirking.

"I have been learning to cook and also to read and write," I replied in a nonchalant way. I suddenly wondered if I was to be abandoned to this life, which I knew did *not* suit me.

"Sadly I've come to take you away from your lessons." Was there a twinkle in his eye? "We are to go south."

"All of us?" I indicated my lord too.

"No, just you and I." He lowered his voice, though the door was shut. "The King is back. He has established a base at Winchester, but needs to secure the south, so it is still unsafe for his sons to reveal themselves. We go to seek news."

I was thrilled – some action at last.

"London will be stubborn," my lord intervened. "The Danes have it in their grip."

"So it may be some time before we can bring you *good* news," Ealdwine answered him.

We set off towards Winchester. Others of my lord's

household were with us and, thankfully, there were enough horses for us all. I didn't ask them where they'd been hiding for we all understood that the less we knew the better. If something went wrong, my lord would still be safe.

I think we were somewhere near Newbury when we got news that the King had moved to Guildford.

"It looks as though his sights are set on London," Ealdwine commented, as we turned to go east.

When we finally caught up with the court, I expected the King to enquire after his sons, but nothing was said, well, not in my presence. We were fed and given places to sleep, but the King appeared very distracted.

We all ate in a large hall, presumably at the home of some thegn though I can't remember his name. Ealdwine kept me by his side much of the time, as I think he felt responsible for me. He managed to pick up bits of news, which he shared while we ate.

I looked around the hall. I recognised earl Eadric and decided he must still be in the King's confidence. But I also noticed a Danish clique, with Thorkell among them.

"Father Ealdwine, I recognise Thorkell the Tall," I said. "He's still serving the King?"

"Yes, he went into exile in Normandy, but has returned with him to help him regain the kingdom. His fleet is moored at the mouth of the Thames, but can't get upriver because London is well guarded."

"I've spotted another group who don't look English,"

I told him. "On the other side, not with the Danes. But maybe they are Danes too for they are fair and dress like Danes."

Ealdwine followed my eyes, saw the group I meant and then returned to eating.

"The leader is the stout one," he said quietly.

I glanced across and spotted a man almost as broad as he was tall. If he had stood next to Thorkell, I reckoned he would hardly reach his chest, but he looked strong, rippling with muscles in his arms.

"Who is he?" I whispered.

"Olaf Haraldson. His nickname is Olaf the Stout – and you can see why." Ealdwine smiled. "He's from Norway, not Denmark."

"What's he doing here?"

"The King picked him up while in exile," the priest explained. "He'd already got Thorkell, but he found Olaf was at a loose end, so he's employed him too. They're not cheap. The English will be paying for them in raised taxes."

That didn't sound good to me, but I supposed the King wanted some fearsome fighters in order to regain his kingdom.

"Do they get on?" I asked.

"Who?"

"Thorkell and Olaf."

"They campaigned together against our nation a few years ago and have come to support our King completely independently, but it might be an uneasy relationship for there's no love lost between Norway and Denmark. Norway doesn't want to be lorded over by its little southern neighbour. They could make strange bedfellows here in Aethelred's pay – that's what links them – money. They might go off and fight for someone else if they get a better offer."

"Both of them?"

"Olaf became a Christian in Normandy, I think through the influence of the King and Queen, so I don't think he'd go – not just yet. Thorkell? Who knows? He might stick with our King, as Cnut's untried and Thorkell has never fought for Cnut. But they're both Danes. Nationality might prove stronger than money, especially if Cnut offers more."

I didn't find the news cheerful. The King seemed to be depending on two foreign forces, who wouldn't naturally be fighting on the same side anyway. These foreigners could suddenly decide to join the enemy, fight each other or simply leave us. The other major cause for concern was London. None of us realised then how that would be resolved.

CHAPTER 9

Soon the court moved to Richmond, but we had to stay on the southern side of the Thames as there was no bridge between Staines and Southwark. Our fleet was beyond London and even the smaller vessels couldn't come up to Richmond because London itself was a formidable barrier. At least, this was what I was hearing and I wanted to see for myself. So when there was a rumour of an exploration to test the enemy's strength, I determined to be part of it.

A lad like me can always be of use. We can run errands and take messages, we can carry baggage and we can look after horses, amongst other things. So I wormed my way into this advance party.

There were a couple of local thegns who knew the territory and quite a gang of English, but there was also Thorkell the Dane and Olaf the Norwegian and some of their fighters.

We kept well to the south and skirted round Southwark. On the journey I made friends with a young man from London called Leofric, who'd chosen to go into exile rather than be ruled by a Dane.

"I know there's a bridge," I said, "because I've been over it. It's big, isn't it?"

"Massive," Leofric agreed. "Two wagons wide. It's built of timber, but strong."

"The Danes control it?"

"Oh yes and the settlement of Southwark to the south.

We're on our way to see how heavily it's defended."

What we found was depressing. Towers – timber and insubstantial, but numerous – had been built on the bridge itself and from these towers archers could easily shoot down at any boats trying to pass under the bridge. As for Southwark and London, we found both defended by fresh banks of wood and earth, difficult for an attacker to scale. London looked even more impregnable than when I had been there the previous summer, so I reckoned we faced an even more difficult situation than Swein had faced.

We camped at a safe distance and set up guards in case any Danes thought to attack us, but those behind the walls stayed behind the walls and didn't risk a battle.

The discussion around the evening fire was animated, though much of it I couldn't understand as Olaf and Thorkell were doing most of the talking.

"Do you know what they're saying?" I asked Leofric.

"No, they talking Norse, but I get the impression Olaf has some kind of plan, though Thorkell is sceptical."

The next day some of the Danish boats were brought upriver to near Greenwich. I say 'Danish', but really I don't know if they were Thorkell's and they could just as easily have been Olaf's. Certainly it was Olaf who appeared to be in charge of what happened next.

I was grabbed to help dismantle a nearby barn and take out the wattle panels between the timbers. The daub was crumbling away, but the interlaced pieces of wood were still intact. We had to carry these down to the river, where we found others had cut some willow and were repairing any gaps and also weaving the pieces together. I was totally mystified as to what was going on. It almost looked as though they were making wooden rafts, but I couldn't see how they could float very well.

By midday, I could see that the wickerwork panels were being put on the boats to act as roofs. There was still plenty of room for the men to row beneath these canopies, which actually stuck out beyond the sides of the boats.

"It's not raining, so it can't be to stop the rowers getting wet," I commented to Leofric. "Any ideas?"

"No, but I think Olaf definitely has a plan. This could be exciting. Look, the tide's rising."

The water level was definitely coming up. Leofric was dragged away to take part in some discussion, and when he returned, he gave me a broad grin.

"They were asking about high tide," he told me. "They're going to row up on the full tide. I'm not sure what for, but shall we follow?"

I hadn't come this far to miss the action, and as long as we stayed out of range of any arrows, we reckoned we could be safe.

The Danes had piled into the boats and were preparing to row upriver, so that left quite a contingent of English to keep pace with them along the bank.

"Keep pace" we couldn't, as the boats moved much faster than we did. We could see them getting very near the bridge. The enemy shot arrows at them, but the canopies protected them and soon the boats were actually under the bridge, where they stopped.

"What are they doing?" Leofric asked. "Can you see?"

I'd noticed the boats had thick ropes in them when they set off and I thought these were now being used.

"They've got the ropes out!" I exclaimed. "Look! I think they're tying them round the wooden piles that support the bridge."

"Yes! I see it! I think you're right!" he agreed. "Now what?"

Because they were actually under the bridge and the bridge was so broad, they could work without too much danger, for the enemy couldn't get them in its sights. Even so, it was a very dangerous situation and I admired the bravery of these men.

"The tide's turning," Leofric suddenly said. "They've been working in the slack water, but it's going to run soon."

"So they're not going further?"

"No, I think they're going to come back this way."

"But their boats will be tied to the bridge piles!"

We still didn't understand. Then the boats began to drift downriver and the arrows fell on them again, but either stuck in the wickerwork or bounced off into the water. Soon the rowers were out of range and gathering speed.

Then we realised the nature of the plan.

The men were now rowing furiously and I could see the ropes they'd attached to the piles dragging in the water. Then one by one the boats juddered and slowed and the rowers braced themselves to row even harder. The ropes were taut.

There was a scream of broken wood as the first pile was dislodged and a scream from men on the banks either side. We shouted our encouragement to the rowers and they pulled even harder on their oars. Another pile was dislodged and then another.

On the bridge itself, I think there was panic. They couldn't really see what was happening because it was underneath. All they could hear was the breaking of the wooden supports and yet there seemed to be no effort to get off the bridge.

Suddenly one of the timber towers collapsed and spilled its archers down into the river. Then another pile was dislodged and a top section disintegrated, causing more people to fall into the water.

The boats were almost stationary despite the efforts of the rowers, but help was at hand for more boats came upriver to join them. They threw ropes round the raised sterns and secured them to their own prows. Then the second group of rowers got to work. Now there were two boats pulling on each of the timbers.

The whole bridge was beginning to tremble and the shifting crowd on it added to its instability. Another pile went and another tower. We cheered ourselves hoarse, even though there were men fighting for their lives in the cold, murky water and being pulled under by the ebbing tide.

One last effort on the part of the rowers caused the final piles to fall. The bridge gave a last shudder and collapsed.

What a sight! I don't think I'll ever forget that.

The next day the King arrived with a fighting force and very quickly received the submission of Southwark, for without the bridge it had, literally, lost the support of London. I thought London would take longer to bring to heel, but then I realised the situation was not the same as it had been for us last year. Even when Swein came against us, we still had our link to the outside world, for we controlled the lower part of the Thames and Thorkell had his fleet moored at Greenwich. This time London had no outside link. Yes, they had substantial walls, but I guessed the food supplies would be under pressure. We had been besieged in the autumn after a good harvest, but they faced a siege in March when food was short.

Two days after Olaf's men had caused the bridge to collapse, they could celebrate their triumph fully – for London submitted.

When I met up with Ealdwine, I had much to tell him.

"It's sad that so many died," he sighed. "War is a terrible thing. If only our land could be at peace and English and Dane could live together."

"We'll never live with them!" I declared.

"I think we'll have to learn to," was his response. "And now there may be more killing, for the King will go against the north."

"Do you think that will submit as easily as London?" I asked.

He shook his head.

"I doubt it. Some of the lords may decide to return to the King now Swein's dead and the King holds London and the south. But there is much bitterness among the people there."

I thought back to my time in York and knew he was right. People like Ufegeat wouldn't want the King, but I wasn't sure how influential he was. As a blinded man, he'd been unable to take on the mantle of his father. There were other lords, most of whom I'd never met, and they would be the ones who'd decide whether to submit or fight.

The next day Ealdwine told me we were leaving.

"We're going to take the news back to lord Edmund. He and his brother need to be with the King again."

"So they'll come to London?"

"No. The King is planning to march north with a force."

We travelled as fast as we could, stopping at Winchcombe to give a report to lord Athelstan, who promptly decided to join us in our journey to Evesham.

"This is wonderful news!" My lord Edmund was delighted. "London, Wessex, Mercia – they are all ours.

Brother, I plan to join our father and fight with him."

"So do I. This is a great opportunity for us to fight together."

Thus we left the monastery and went to the home of earl Leofwine. The monks must have wondered what had happened to us. Maybe they guessed, but I think it's more likely they never realised the true identity of my lord Edmund – that was just as well, as the future was still uncertain.

Earl Leofwine had been among those who'd welcomed back the King, though in my hearing nothing was said about his grandson, whose life as a hostage was now in great danger. The earl, however, made us welcome and messengers were sent to gather all the household members of both aethelings. My lord was happy to be reunited with his sword and fighting gear.

Once assembled, we moved east and met up with the King and his force at Hertford.

"Athelstan, my son!" the King exclaimed, throwing his arms round him. "You are alive and well, praise God!"

My lord Edmund stood quietly by, watching this reunion.

"And Edmund too." The King merely nodded in his direction.

The King had managed to assemble quite an army to take north including Thorkell and Olaf and some of their men, but there were no boats apparently. The plan seemed to be to sweep through the land.

"The word from Gainsborough," I heard the King telling his sons, "is that the men of the north will gather round Cnut after Easter. But we aren't going to wait. We hope to catch them unprepared."

It sounded as though the King had spies in the enemy camp and, when I thought about it, I realised that must be the case. Perhaps Cnut had spies here in the King's court and I looked around sometimes to see if I could spot a traitor, but, of course, any spy would be just like us – that was how they operated.

We soon moved north, and near Huntingdon we met with a force from East Anglia led by lord Ulfketel, but he came in peace, not to fight but to back our cause. I didn't see the meeting between the King and his errant son-in-law, but I heard there had been angry words on the part of the King and pleas for mercy on the part of the earl. So that was one more lord safely back in the fold.

Two more were brought to heel at Stamford. This town was one of the Five Boroughs which came under the lordship of Morcar and Siferth. I had met earl Siferth the previous summer, a rotund and jolly man and unlike his brother Morcar, who was lean and haggard.

We all worshipped together on Palm Sunday and I noticed the pretty lady Frida was with her husband. We ate together later that day – no meat, of course, but better food than we'd had for a while and certainly better than I'd had in the monastery.

My lord Athelstan was seated by earl Morcar and they were in deep and serious conversation. Earl Ulfketel sat by the King, but neither appeared to say much. The earl of Mercia was not with us and I supposed he had returned to his family after being in exile.

My lord Edmund was next to the lady Frida and as I was close by ready to refill his cup and meet any other need, I caught snatches of their conversation.

"Your brother-in-law does not look well and I see his wife is not here," my lord commented.

"Morcar is pained in spirit more than in body," she replied and paused. "He has lost Ealdgyth," she added quietly.

"You mean she's died?"

She nodded.

"She was with child, but miscarried and bled to death."

"I'm so sorry."

"They have a young daughter, but Morcar has been hit hard."

My lord was quiet.

"Remind me," he said at length. "Ealdgyth, she was related to the late earl Aelfhelm, wasn't she?"

"His niece and therefore cousin to Wulfheah, Ufegeat and Aelfgifu."

"And Aelfgifu is now the wife of Cnut."

"That does not mean we are supporters of Danish rule," she declared. "I know my husband and Morcar submitted, but ... life is complicated up here in the north."

She turned her head very slightly and gave my lord a look that I think was full of meaning though I couldn't read it.

"I heard," my lord began after a while, "I heard terrible accounts of Danish acts of barbarism." He took a drink and I thought his hand was shaking. "I heard the wives of thegns, well, at least one such woman, had been grossly defiled." He was definitely shaking now. "I pray you were left unharmed by them."

"I was, my lord. Be assured, there was no such defilement here in the north. The lords submitted quickly and Swein respected their families. Down south, that was different. I hear there was resistance, so the account of ... of defilement is probably from the south. I was unharmed."

"Praise God!" was his response and his whole body relaxed.

The next day we were on the move again. A messenger had come with news to anger the King, so I kept well out of his way. Ealdwine knew what had happened though.

"The King sent to the earl of Lindsey and asked him to submit," the priest told me, "but he has scorned the request." He sighed. "You know what that means?"

I shook my head.

"It means the force now goes north with one purpose," he grimaced. "To kill. There'll be no mercy."

CHAPTER 10

I guessed our target was Gainsborough, as that was meant to be Cnut's stronghold, though whether he was actually there was anyone's guess, for rumours were circulating that he had been leading parties of fighting men out and about to keep the locals in submission. Now these people would be caught between two forces, both determined to crush the other.

We moved north as a unit, but could go no faster than most of the fighters who were on foot. They carried a variety of weapons, but many had some sort of seax, with its vicious power to cut. My lord made me travel with Ealdwine, near the rear, for I was not yet of an age to wield a weapon, though I had begun to practise, in the hope of developing strong muscles. In the meantime, I was useful as an armour carrier, though after just one day's travelling, I was relieved of that, for my lord took to wearing his mail shirt and had his sword slung about him.

It was near Lincoln where we had the first action. A village had sent its women and children into hiding and now its men sought to defend it. The King demanded provisions, but he was refused. The men were cut down, their homes and barns raided and then set alight.

As the force moved on, Ealdwine lingered and went among the dying, giving them the last rites. When we had gone, we knew the women would creep back to bury them.

Of course, they weren't Danes – they were English, just like us.

We heard Cnut was in the east of Lindsey, so we turned east. Villages which did not welcome us received the same barbarity as I had witnessed before. Some claimed all their supplies had been taken by the Danes, but the King still ordered their destruction. We left behind us grieving widows and plumes of smoke. It was a sad day's work and we still hadn't found the enemy.

The next day word came that there was a force just south of Grimsby which was moving west, so we turned to head them off and I came close to my first battle.

Being at the rear and left in charge of my lord's horse, for men in those days fought on foot (we have changed our ways since), I couldn't see much of what happened. Even Ealdwine left me, for he said his place was ministering to the dying.

The King wore a helmet, mail coat and sword, but he also had his bodyguard, an elite who were to protect him if need be. The aethelings had no such group, but they had their war gear and their swords were polished, ready for action.

It is the noise that I remember – the shouting, the clashing of shields and the screams. I guessed the shouting was insults thrown across by both sides as they lined up behind their shields. The land was flat, so no one had a terrain advantage as each side edged forward. Then came the screams as swords met flesh and shields failed to protect, and men slipped in the mud and the blood, and were trampled on.

Those two hours seemed a lifetime, but our force was too strong for them and even from where I stood I could sense the break-up of the battle and men beginning to flee and I guessed we had won the day, though at what cost? Was my lord hurt?

He came to me at last, blood on his mail coat and stinking of sweat.

"My lord, are you alright?"

"Yes, Wulfgar." He looked at his gory hands. "I've killed a few men today, but I've no wound."

"We've won?"

"As much as one ever wins a battle," he grimaced. "Some will never fight again and those who've survived will be forced to bow the knee."

"And Cnut? Was he here?"

"No, damn him! The force was led by the earl of Lindsey. Cnut's somewhere else."

"Will the earl now submit?"

My lord looked at me and I tried to read his face.

"He can't," he said simply. "My father killed him."

I wasn't sure if he meant he'd killed him in the battle or executed him after taking him a prisoner. I rather suspect it was the latter, for the King was in no mood for mercy.

We camped nearby and the light was failing before I met up again with Ealdwine. He too had blood on his clothes, though he had washed any from his hands.

"This is Holy Week," he said sadly, "and we are killing our fellow English men."

"Have many died?" I asked.

"Too many," was all he would say, as he gazed into the firelight and crumbled a piece of bread between his fingers, without making any effort to eat it.

There was nothing I could say. He was a priest and would rather be praising God than witnessing such needless bloodshed. Well, it was needless in his eyes, but I thought the only way to peace was to crush the opposition with force.

"I have been praying with the injured too," he told me. "Lord Athelstan took a blow to his arm, but there is a woman skilled with herbs who has dressed the wound."

"Our lord is unscathed," I boasted.

He gave me a wry smile.

"I think he was born with a sword in his hand," he commented.

The next morning I was helping my lord to dress when Ealdwine came in with news.

"A messenger has come to the King from earl Uhtred."

"Is the news good or bad?" asked my lord swiftly.

"Good, I hope," the priest answered. "He craves mercy of the King and says he will hold the area north of York for him, but he cannot bring his force to join ours, for the Humber is in the hands of Cnut."

"And did my father rant and rave or was he sensible?"

"Earl Ulfketel was with him and that helped, for earl Uhtred only asked what earl Ulfketel had and how could the King be merciful to one of his sons-in-law and not to the other?"

My lord grunted.

"So I think he has been ... perhaps not forgiven, but reprieved," Ealdwine concluded.

"I hope that's so. Uhtred is a good man and I wouldn't want to see him stabbed in the back once he was back in my father's favour."

Ealdwine said nothing and I was able to continue with dressing my lord for war.

"Any news of my brother?"

"He's in good spirits, but won't be wielding a sword today."

"Right. I'm ready. Now to find that damned Dane and teach him a lesson!"

That was indeed the aim. We had, literally, eliminated the earl of Lindsey, now we needed to do the same to Cnut, then York could easily be recovered because of earl Uhtred's change of heart.

We marched west towards Gainsborough, any recalcitrant villages suffering the fate of others we had already destroyed. There was no battle that day and our scouts had no news of an enemy force. We would reach Gainsborough the next day it was reckoned. Would we find it heavily defended like London? We had no ships to make an assault on a vital bridge this time.

Ealdwine was quietly weeping that evening.

"Father, whatever is the matter?" I whispered, not wanting others to see his distress.

"This night, Christ ate with his disciples," he said, wiping his eyes, but not looking at me. "Then he prayed in the garden before being betrayed." He leaned closer and added, "I'm going to spend the night in prayer. I doubt my lord will need me."

He got up and slipped away from the firelight, leaving me to wonder about our mission. The next day was a very holy day when we should be remembering Christ's death on the cross, but we would be out killing Englishmen if we couldn't find any Danes to kill. But I couldn't see we had any option.

We reached Gainsborough before midday and the King sent a delegation to demand surrender. We expected to besiege the town and were preparing to surround it if we could, when word came that the gates were open.

A buzz ran through the army, but men were wary. Was it some trick? Forth from the gates came the leading men of the town and knelt on the track before the King. Word of what happened next was passed through the troops.

"Where is Cnut?" the King had demanded.

"Gone," they had replied. "He left with his ships two days ago."

Two days ago? That was before we had beaten the

force led by the earl of Lindsey! Cnut had run and he'd left his allies to be thrashed.

So England was back in our hands and the King again ruled the whole land from Northumbria to Hampshire, Shropshire to East Anglia. The Danish dog was retreating with his tail between his legs. We were euphoric!

We celebrated Easter in York – in style! Earl Uhtred and his wife, the King's daughter, were also here, so all seemed well. Our nation was united again. One thing troubled me though.

"Father," I asked Ealdwine, "is there any news of the hostages Swein took last year?"

He sighed.

"Wulfgar, you are right to ask," he acknowledged. "No one is talking about them and that is not because they have been released, but because Cnut has taken them with him."

"Oh, no! Why?"

"I guess he needed to be sure of a safe passage back to Denmark for he has nowhere else to go," Ealdwine suggested. "If our ships had come up and blocked the Humber, he could have used them as a bargaining tool."

"But our ships are still near London, aren't they?"

"We know that, but Cnut didn't or else he may have been told by spies, but still been unsure. As it is, he's got the hostages on board."

"What will he do?" My imagination was running riot.

"You are right to look fearful for he could slit their

throats and throw them overboard." He paused and gave a deep sigh. "We may never know their fate, though I pray they will live."

"Father, you prayed all night before we reached Gainsborough and the town was taken without a fight. Was that an answer to prayer?"

"Perhaps." He smiled a rare smile. "I have been crying out for peace and ... well, here we are ... in York on Easter Day, the day of resurrection, the day of new life. I do pray this means a fresh start for our country."

CHAPTER 11

We stayed in York for several days as it was important to ensure that the whole region was now back under the King's control. One person I didn't see was Ufegeat and his young guide Ulf and I guessed he was keeping well out of the way.

My lord and his brother were in good spirits and I felt things were looking up after all the trauma of the last nine months. When the King decided to return to London, we made a more leisurely journey south, spending a few days with earl Siferth in Derbyshire. Earl Morcar was there too and looked less haggard; he was obviously enjoying the company of the King's sons. Lord Athelstan was still troubled by the wound he had received, so we were all thankful the fighting was over – at least for the time being. There had been no news of Cnut and we presumed he'd returned to Denmark.

After we left Derbyshire, my lord decided on a detour to Evesham, so we bade farewell to lord Athelstan's party for they were going back to his home in Wessex.

"I wish to thank Abbot Aelfric for sheltering us, Wulfgar," he told me, "and I will take an offering for his monastery."

So the two of us went into the abbey, where the abbot welcomed us warmly.

"We have been praying that peace might return to our country," the cleric said, "and it seems our prayers have been answered."

"You need to pray now that my father keeps all the promises he made," my lord warned. "Not everyone is pleased he's back in power."

The abbot turned to me.

"Wulfgar, there is someone I wish your lord to meet. He's in our infirmary for we are ... caring for him at present. Please ask him to come to my room. And when you have done that, you can go and talk to the monks in the kitchen."

I sped off and it wasn't until I reached the door of the infirmary that I realised I didn't know which patient I had to ask for.

In the room were a few beds, two of which had sleeping occupants. The monk in charge recognised me.

"Wulfgar! What a surprise! Are you back with us?"

"No, it's just a visit – to say thank you for giving us sanctuary." I thought it best to say no more. "The abbot says you have a patient I should take to him."

I looked around, a little puzzled.

"Ah," said the monk, "that will be Aethelwine. He's in the garden. I'll take you to him."

He led me out to the herb garden where the scents of May were filling the air and the bees were busy on the rosemary bushes. A man was seated in the sunshine, but he had his back to us and a hood over his head.

"Aethelwine, the abbot has sent this lad to say he wishes to see you."

The man turned and I gasped.

"I know, lad," the youthful patient said, "I look a bit of a mess."

I stared at his face, speechless.

"The Danes cut off my nose," he explained, "but at least they didn't slit my throat."

"I'm ... I'm sorry," I stuttered.

His hood slipped back a little and I saw to my horror that his ears had also been cut off. He got up.

"Abbot Aelfric wants me, does he?"

I nodded.

"Then we'd better obey," he concluded.

Although his face was disfigured, his eyes still twinkled.

"Lead on," he ordered.

I walked ahead of him, trying to get my head round what had happened. Somehow the Danes had caught him and done this to him, but hadn't killed him.

When we reached the abbot's room, I turned.

"He told me just to bring you," I explained.

"Thank you, but you'll have to knock the door for me." He looked down. "I don't have any hands."

My eyes followed his and I realised that the ends of his arms were bandaged.

"The Danes cut those off too," he added.

I made a feeble attempt at knocking the door, but my hand didn't want to work. I'm afraid he must have seen the shock on my face.

When the abbot said "Come in", I opened the door, let the patient in and fled. I felt sick. I didn't go straight to the kitchen; I couldn't face talking to anyone at all for a few minutes.

My lord later found me loitering in the cloisters and we walked together to the gatehouse.

"Do you know who that man was that the abbot wanted me to meet?" he asked.

"His name was Aethelwine," I replied.

"Does that mean anything?"

"I don't think so," I confessed.

"You remember earl Leofwine. Well, that's his grandson," my lord explained. "He was given to Swein as a hostage last year, when Swein captured Mercia."

"Oh." I was beginning to remember.

"Cnut took all the hostages with him when we recaptured the north," he continued.

He looked at me sideways as we walked.

"You saw what they did to him?"

"Yes."

"He told me Cnut took all the hostages south with him and let them disembark at Sandwich before he sailed for Denmark." He grunted. "Of course, he had to make some kind of statement, so all of them had their noses, ears and hands cut off."

I was silent.

"The locals helped them to return to their homes, so he's here until his wounds heal, which I pray they will."

"He could have killed them," I said quietly, recalling Aethelwine seemed glad to have survived.

"If he'd killed them and thrown them in the sea, we wouldn't know about it," my lord responded. "Because they are alive, they are living examples of what happens if you cross Cnut." He grunted again. "Damn that man and every Dane who tries to take our land."

I knew he meant it. Meeting Aethelwine had touched my lord deeply I could tell, for his buoyant air left him for the rest of our journey back to our base south-west of Newbury. Once home, he was less gloomy for there was work to do after such a long absence. The homestead had survived the Danish incursion, but those left to run the estate had been slack in their duties and now had to attend to matters they'd let slip.

My lord was out and about, checking fences, hedges and ditches and ordering an overhaul of the machinery in the mill. He chided the shepherd for lambs needlessly lost and told off the woodsmen for their negligence of pollarding.

May slipped into June and the days were long and busy. He got me counting the fleeces from the shorn sheep and I was then shown how to divide these between those going to London for sale and those to be spun locally. Those to be traded were weighed and bundled, but those being kept had special treatment.

"We grease them, see," the shepherd explained. "We use lard. It helps separate the fibres and then we combs them with teasel heads."

I had a vague idea about spinning and weaving, but as part of the aetheling's household I now had to find out more, so the shepherd showed me how the hooks on the seed heads of the teasel plants acted like combs, pulling the strands of wool free of each other.

"Now we takes it to the spinners," he told me, and I had to help carry some of the wool to a house in the village, where a toothless woman showed me how she worked magic with her spindle.

Then the shepherd took me to another house where a loom stood against one of the inside walls. A woman harassed by two lively children was making broth, but then she broke off her task to demonstrate how she worked the spun wool across the wefts with a shuttle, the warps being held vertical by stones pierced through with holes.

"They be loom weights," the shepherd explained. "She can work on this piece of cloth and cook and care for the children, all at the same time." He glanced at her. "But it be hard work," he added, and the woman nodded.

"Do we sell the cloth?" I asked.

"Some of it be sold and some kept for us. English cloth be known throughout the world, for our sheep be the best," he boasted.

I was beginning to realise how many people depended on the homestead for their livelihood. It wasn't just those of us who lived with my lord, but also people in the village, those spinners and weavers.

It felt good that now the Danes had gone we could get on with our normal lives. None of us realised something quite different would disturb the usual pattern.

As well as the less exciting jobs such as dealing with wool, I was allowed some training in how to fight. Archery was one of the skills I had to practise and I liked my time at the butts and being taught how arrows were made. I would pretend the bull's eye was the nose of a Dane, for the image of Aethelwine's mutilated face never quite left me. I was also beginning to be fairly useful with a seax and knew that one day I would be tall enough and strong enough to wield a proper sword.

On the 20th day of June, it being a Sunday, we celebrated the feast of St. Alban, and Ealdwine told us the story of how a man had saved a Christian priest like him from the sword of the Roman occupiers, but how he had then been condemned to death in his place.

"He was led up the hill to be executed," Ealdwine narrated, "but the executioner could not carry out the dastardly deed for he saw that Alban was a holy man."

I always liked the next bit.

"So he said he would die with Alban," the story continued. "Another man proudly stepped forward and said he would wield the axe, but he paid a huge price for his boast, for as he did the terrible deed, his eyes fell out."

We all clapped and said it served him right and Ealdwine finished by recounting miracles done by the saint after his death. We feasted on meat and mead and enjoyed the long days of summer unaware our cosy life was about to be shattered.

Two days later, a rider galloped into the homestead with an urgent message.

"Lord Athelstan is desperately ill and has called for his brother to go to him!"

CHAPTER 12

We reached the homestead on the Wednesday evening and were met by the seneschal.

"Aelfmaer, how's my brother?" my lord asked, hurriedly dismounting.

"Not good." The man shook his head. "I fear it will not be long."

"He can't die!" my lord cried. "Surely something can be done?"

"We've tried many remedies, but all to no avail. The wound has never healed and we fear the poison is everywhere in his body now."

"Take me to him."

I stayed to help with the horses and unpacking our goods. Another of lord Athelstan's retainers showed us where we would sleep. I noticed Ealdwine was holding the cross that hung round his neck and his lips were moving. I guessed he was silently praying.

Eventually we went into the hall where food had been put for us, though none of us felt like eating much. It was some time before we were joined by our lord, who seated himself next to Ealdwine.

"The situation is very grave," he said quietly.

"He has his priest with him?" Ealdwine enquired.

"Yes, Aelfwine's there." He paused. "He's feverish, but lucid enough. He's made his will."

Those words hung in the air like smoke trapped in a

small room – invading us, suffocating us, stinging our eyes. My mouth was dry and I wondered if my heart still beat.

"He has sent to our father," my lord continued, "for he needs his permission for some of the grants he has made. God, this is awful!"

He put his head in his hands, but he did not weep. None of us knew what to say.

The next day my lord spent all his time with his brother and I was left to make myself useful. That wasn't easy because the whole place was quiet and little was happening. Lord Athelstan's retainers got on with their usual tasks, though I did find Aelfnoth sitting in the shade, staring across the yard, a sword at his side. I crouched by him and he turned and gave me a slight nod.

"Feel like polishing a sword?" he muttered.

"I will if you like," I responded.

He picked up the sword, but laid it across his knees with no attempt to pass it to me.

"He's given me this," he said quietly.

I could see it was a fine sword for the blade was notched where it had met resistance and the handle was inlaid with niello.

"He's left it to me in his will," he added. "He's not going to need it where he's going and he's not going to need my services either."

"What happens ..." I wasn't sure I should ask, "... to the household when someone dies?"

115

"We lose our lord." He paused. "We lose our home." He sighed deeply. "Maybe your lord will need me," he added and tried to smile.

"I hope so. I'm rubbish at sword-polishing." I hoped to cheer him by my comment, but I don't think he heard me.

"His slaves will be freed, so they can start a new life," he continued. "Some of his men will probably get grants of land and that will give them an income. We'll have to find new lords if we're to live."

It felt like the homestead was already wrapped in the death shroud and there was very little talking when we ate together that evening. There were two new faces I didn't recognise.

"Father," I whispered to Ealdwine, "who are those men?"

He followed my eyes before looking back at his plate.

"The older one is Bishop Aelfsige of Winchester," he told me. "Lord Athelstan has asked to be buried at the Old Minster there. The other is the local abbot. With Father Aelfwine, they'll take it in turns to pray through the night with lord Athelstan." He paused. "He's not at peace."

"What do you mean?" I was puzzled.

"He's fighting death," Ealdwine explained. "I don't think it's fear of dying, for he's been shrived and is ready to face God. But he's waiting to hear from his father."

I looked across at my lord Edmund. His face was pale and his eyes weary. He looked as though he had shrunk a couple of inches. I don't think he'd slept much since we got the news.

The Friday was another warm oppressive day. Perhaps, under different circumstances, it would have felt like joyous midsummer, but we hardly noticed the butterflies that flitted among the flowers in the herb garden. An aetheling's life was nearing its end and there was no joy in that.

Around midday, I was in the yard when some horsemen galloped in.

"Are you from the King?" I shouted.

"Yes!"

"I'll tell them!"

Time was precious, so I ran to the room where I knew lord Athelstan lay and knocked on the door. His priest opened it.

"Men have come from the King," I whispered.

Aelfwine left the door ajar and relayed the news to lord Athelstan, whose flushed face I glimpsed.

"Praise God," I heard him mutter.

Soon, one of the horsemen came past me and knelt by the bed. He was clutching a parchment.

"I have the King's permission, my lord," he panted.

"Good." His voice was very faint. "We can complete the will."

I pulled the door gently towards me and let it latch, giving them their privacy again and I wandered back outside. I had seen death before, but this felt different. I couldn't say why. It was not *my* lord who was dying, but I just knew our lives would change.

They told me it was very peaceful. He had completed the will and it had been witnessed by the bishop, the abbot, Aelfmaer his seneschal and my lord. The bishop had then anointed him with holy oil and given him some consecrated bread. They had stayed with him, but he had fallen into a deep sleep from which he woke in heaven.

The next day, my lord was grey from lack of sleep and wouldn't talk to anyone. After a while he disappeared and those of us with tasks got on with them. Aelfnoth I found polishing a sword.

"I can't sit around doing nothing," he explained, passing me a cloth. "You can rub up that one."

I took up the sword he indicated.

"They're your lord's," he added.

"Are they? I don't recognise them," I answered.

"His brother gave them to him," he said quietly. "The one I'm polishing belonged to the great King Offa."

I could see how magnificent it was. The one I began to polish wasn't as good though it was still far better than most swords men carried. Its hilt had an interesting design on it, which was pitted and therefore hard to polish well.

"He's left his other brother a silver-hilted sword," Aelfnoth continued. "He's old enough to wield one now."

We worked in silence except for the occasional grunt of disapproval at my poor work.

Later in the day, I was collared for a different task.

"Where's your lord?" Aelfmaer confronted me. "There are matters I need to discuss with him."

"I don't know," I answered.

"Then find him, boy!"

I ran round the homestead looking in all the obvious places. He certainly hadn't taken to his bed and no one remembered seeing him for several hours. He didn't seem to be anywhere.

Then I suddenly thought about the church. Just outside the homestead was a simple thatched building which I guessed was used for worship by the villagers. Could he be in there? I ignored the barking of the guard dogs and trotted down the track towards it.

I tiptoed into the church. My lord was there, prostrate on the rough earth floor, weeping. I ran to find Ealdwine and he hurried with me to the building. He knelt by my lord while I hovered near the doorway.

It was several minutes before my lord could be lifted into a sitting position and even then, he buried his face into Ealdwine's chest and the priest enfolded him in his arms. I sat down and leaned against the doorpost, looking out into the fields and the life of the homestead in the distance, but all I heard were the sobs of my lord.

I have no idea how long we sat like that, but eventually there was quiet.

"You loved him greatly," I heard Ealdwine croon.

Then, after a while, the priest seemed to be quoting scripture.

"'The steadfast love of the Lord never ceases, his mercies never come to an end. They are new every morning. Great is thy faithfulness.' That's the prophet Jeremiah, you know, and he experienced great suffering. God understands, my son."

"Does he?"

I was surprised by the desolate tone of my lord's voice.

"I have lost a dear brother." He paused to blow his nose and clear his throat. "But I realise I have lost something else."

Ealdwine was silent. I guessed he was cradling my lord like a child, but I dared not look their way.

"He was very dear to me." My lord's voice was stronger now. "I was never jealous that he was the eldest." He took a deep breath. "In fact, I realise now that I was happy he would be king – and not me."

Ealdwine remained silent. My lord was struggling to get the words out and I thought he would begin to weep again.

"Ealdwine, it's been a game!" And he broke down.

Minutes passed again before he could resume talking.

"A game, my son?" Ealdwine asked.

"Yes." His voice trembled. "I was the younger brother, not expected to be king. I could play, play with power, but take no responsibility."

The silence was so profound I could hear my own tense breathing.

"But it's not a game now," he almost moaned. "I could be king. The weight of this nation would be on my shoulders. It's too much!"

He wept again, but not for so long this time.

"Perhaps this is your destiny, your calling," his priest counselled. "In the Bible there is a story of a girl called Esther who is a nobody, but finds herself in a position to save all the Jews in exile. She ponders whether God may have put her there for that very moment, for that very time."

His voice became firmer as he addressed my lord.

"You have many gifts, my son," he declared. "God has gifted you as a leader. I have seen it. I have watched you over these many years mature into a man who can carry the nation's burden. You understand the people. You understand the enemy. You ... I fear to say this ... but you command more respect than your father. Maybe God has raised you to this task at this time."

I think my lord was listening, for he made no sound.

"You can be a great king," the priest continued, "but, and this is very important, you must rely on God for your wisdom. He should be your supreme counsellor."

"I never knew myself until now," my lord whispered.

"And self-knowledge will keep you humble, aware of your frailty, aware of your need of God."

CHAPTER 13

Lord Athelstan was buried, as he'd requested, at the Old Minster in Winchester. I thought the King would come, but he didn't. Bishop Aelfsige led the service, which was a very sad affair. My lord didn't weep; I think he had spent himself on the previous Saturday. If anything, he seemed numb, expressionless, perhaps to an outsider uncaring, but I had glimpsed how hard he'd taken his older brother's death. His slumped shoulders spoke loudly.

We stayed on at the homestead for, I guess, there was much to organise. Lord Athelstan's wishes had to be put into effect – though that could take months with regard to the grants of land – and his household needed reorganising.

I bumped into Aelfnoth one morning and he smiled, unexpectedly.

"I've good news," he told me. "Your lord is to become my lord. He's taking me into his household."

"As his sword-polisher?"

"Yes, so, young Wulfgar, you won't have to bother with the polishing anymore."

I was doubly pleased – I liked Aelfnoth and I didn't like sword-polishing.

After a month, my lord announced we were going up to London and Aelfmaer was left in charge of the homestead. A year had passed since we'd been besieged there by Swein. And so much had happened – the King's exile, Swein's death, the King's return, the pulling down of Southwark bridge and the final defeat of the north. These were huge events for our country, but not ones for which a man weeps. An aetheling's death was different.

We settled in to our accommodation and joined with other members of the court in worship at St. Paul's. From what I saw, it didn't appear that the King greeted his son warmly. In fact, as we gathered to leave the building there was an exchange between my lord and his father.

"Don't talk to me of Athelstan," the King was saying. "I grieve too much for his loss."

"I'm doing what I can to fulfil his wishes," my lord responded.

"Yes, the estate at Chalton and his other bequests – deal with them quickly – if you can," the King scoffed. "He was a fine young man. You can never take his place. At least, I have Edward."

The King had swept off leaving my lord abandoned. I sought out Ealdwine and told him what I'd heard.

"Let's see if we can find him," the priest suggested.

My lord was seated in a corner of the empty hall, a cup of ale in his hand, staring at his feet. Ealdwine pulled up a stool and I squatted at a respectful distance.

"My lord," Ealdwine began, "you've seen your father?"

"And much good it did," was the gloomy response. "I don't exist." He looked up at his chaplain. "I've never existed. Athelstan was always the favourite. But I thought ..."

His eyes returned to his feet.

"I thought, maybe, now I am the eldest ... But it seems not. His eyes are set on Edward. I am nothing to him."

"He's grieving. He's lost a precious son."

My lord looked up again.

"You think he'll change?" His tone was sharp. "You think he'll realise he has a son old enough to fight for England?! He treats me as a failure. He can't see I'd ever be fit to rule."

Ealdwine sighed.

"Then you must prove him wrong," he counselled. "Do what you can to keep the Danes at bay and our land prosperous. You are free to travel. You don't have the weight of government restricting you. Use this time to heal the wounds of division and reunite us as a country."

My lord was quiet. I felt sure he was listening.

"The King," Ealdwine whispered, "can't do that, but with God's help *you* can. And will, my lord."

So that's what happened. Very soon we returned to the homestead near Newbury. It was mid July and there was work to be done bringing in the hay harvest – or rather ensuring that others brought in the harvest. The weather was kind, and the grass was cut and dried before a violent storm crushed the stubble. This fodder would keep the livestock fed for the winter, so the barns had to be watertight which meant the thatchers had been busy.

The grain harvest was another month away and supplies of food for humans were dwindling. Aelfnoth told me how some of the very poor would eke out their supplies with herbs scavenged from the hedgerows.

"There's poppy, hemp and darnel," he explained. "They grind up the seeds to mix with the grain. But it's a dangerous harvest."

"Why's that?" I asked. "It sounds a good idea to me."

"Makes them crazy," he muttered. "They see visions, dream dreams and think they're living on clouds. They bang down to earth eventually. Our lord will do what he can for the villagers here to make sure they don't starve, nor need to risk going mad."

Lord Edmund was certainly kept busy ensuring everyone did as they should and none slacked. I noticed how he had a gift of getting alongside each man, talking to him, encouraging him sometimes, making each feel valued. As a result, we all worked harder.

The really busy time was early August when the wheat harvest was ready. The weather had done some damage, but not enough to make us face our greatest fear – famine. All the villagers were involved – some had hand sickles to cut the stalks, while others bound it into sheaves and yet others loaded the carts to bring the grain under cover for threshing. All of us helped.

"Ten hours of darkness but fourteen hours of daylight," Aelfnoth declared. "Every hour is precious."

Once threshed, the grain was taken to the village mill for grinding. The miller had been holding back the water in the mill pond because he knew he would need it to turn the great wheel and produce power to set the stones crushing. Long hours for us meant long hours for him too.

Even so, we still celebrated Lammas and gave thanks to God for the first loaf of the wheat harvest. Our happiness was not destroyed this time by awful news of invasion.

Once my lord was sure much of the grain had been harvested, he left a steward to ensure completion of the task and told us we were soon to travel.

We crossed the Thames and journeyed east, stopping briefly at the homes of thegns. The year before, our travelling had been more leisurely, but I sensed some urgency now and it seemed my lord had more serious conversations with his hosts than I remembered in the past.

When we reached the coast of Essex, my lord was particularly interested in any ways the villagers had of defending themselves against invaders. This, of course, was the coast most likely to be attacked by the Danes.

"Ships," I heard him say one day, "that's what we need – a permanent force guarding our coast. And also some means of communicating between ports, so that if an enemy is sighted, it can be attacked quickly before it lands."

Here was a very different kind of country – flat and

marshy, with sea birds wheeling and screeching – and water everywhere.

"Is this where earl Ulfketel is lord?" I asked.

"He has his base at Norwich, north of here," my lord answered, "but I shall encourage him to mobilise the thegns in this area, for all this water aids our enemies."

I looked at him blankly.

"Think, Wulfgar," he scolded. "How do the Danes travel?"

"In boats."

"Yes, and they need safe harbours for their boats," he added. "Here are rivers and places to anchor – the Crouch, the Blackwater, the Colne, the Stour, the Orwell – a lot of rivers! Too many safe havens for Danish ships."

What a task! I thought. Trying to defend this coastline, but that's why we were here, I guessed, so that my lord could think about a strategy. His father had made a complete mess of mobilising a fleet. My lord hoped to be a different kind of leader.

We spent some time with earl Ulfketel before we moved west and came to an even more watery area. They told me it was called the Fens, and we had local guides to show us the way through, as the safe tracks were often obscure.

"This would be a good place to hide," I commented to Aelfnoth.

"Ah, place is full of men who've escaped the law," he informed me. "It gives me the creeps. Fen dens I call it.

127

Thieves and outlaws everywhere."

After that I kept an eye open for fear of ambush, but we were a well-armed party and came through to the area near the Wash without mishap.

By now it was late September and there was a chill wind blowing from the east which found its way in through every crack in the hall where we were staying. During the night, I lay awake, hearing the thatch moaning and the shutters groaning. A bucket out in the yard was rolled across the cobbles, its wooden sides thumping against the stones. A dog whimpered, so I knew I was not the only one awake.

The next morning, we had hardly left our beds before a messenger threw open the hall door.

"Escape – as fast as you can!" he cried.

CHAPTER 14

There was panic in the hall. I grabbed my seax, thinking we were being attacked by bandits, while others slung their swords round their waists.

"What's happening?" cried lord Edmund, unsheathing his sword.

"The sea!" shouted the messenger. "There's a great tide and waves like mountains!"

We fled from the hall, saddled up our horses, piled our goods on a wagon and took the road west – along with everyone else from the homestead and all the villagers too. At least the wind was at our backs, but it seemed to hiss and snarl like a wild beast. Could we outrun the water? I hardly dared look back.

Even the wind could not silence the sound of the dogs barking and the children crying. To me it felt like the end of the world was coming, and I was scared. But my lord had a cool head in the crisis and instead of galloping off into the distance, he kept stopping to check no one was in trouble. He had ordered several of the party to carry children with them on the horses.

"Wulfgar!" he shouted. "There's a woman here about to collapse! Get her into the cart!"

The old lady was wheezing and breathless, clutching her chest as though she had no air in her lungs. I dismounted and, with some help, managed to get her up into our wagon, where she slumped down exhausted.

I looked back as I remounted. I couldn't see the water, but I sensed it, running towards us, wanting to drown us. I spurred on my horse.

About midday the wind seemed to ease. We had come to a halt on what the locals called a hill, but to me it seemed no higher than the rest of the land. We rested and there was some sharing of such bread and ale as had been rescued before we left. Again my lord prowled around, seeking out any in need.

Aelfnoth nudged my arm.

"Can you see it?" he asked, pointing east.

"I can't see anything," I admitted. "It's all grey. Am I looking at sea or sky?"

"Sea."

My eyes roamed across the landscape.

"It's covered the fields all across there," he told me. "There's not a house to be seen either."

"Are we safe here?" I found I was shivering.

"The locals say this is the highest ground for quite a way. Better pray the tide turns soon."

It did, but the water was reluctant to retreat. The fields were sodden and the tracks muddy streams. We had to camp out where we were and do our best to keep warm. In the afternoon the clouds crumpled apart and a weak sun managed to raise our spirits.

"We have a home to go to," Aelfnoth muttered, "but for most of these folk, there'll be no village to return to."

"At least they have their lives," I responded. "I

wonder if anyone has drowned out there."

"Most likely," was his sad response. "No one's ever seen a flood like this."

Eventually we were able to resume our journey and we slowly came to Stamford, but everywhere we heard news of the devastation the great tide had caused. We sheltered with earl Morcar.

"I hope you can do something for the people who've suffered," I overheard my lord saying to the earl. "There are whole villages to the east of here which have been swept away."

"I will do what I can," the earl agreed. "We can get supplies of timber from our woods, but a very real problem will be the water."

"Contaminated by salt?"

"Many wells and pools will have been ruined, but then, I don't suppose much livestock has survived so the need for drinking water isn't great for the present. The harvest was in, but what's happened to that now?" The earl shrugged his shoulders. "That's ruined too."

"So supplies of food will be needed for many months," my lord asserted. "Is your brother in the area?"

"Further north I believe," earl Morcar answered. "I expect we'll work together on this."

My lord was quiet for a while.

"Then I'll leave soon," he said at length, "and go south to mobilise other thegns to help."

Over the coming days, we worked our way south

131

through Northampton and Aylesbury, and everywhere my lord did what he could to persuade the thegns to help the communities which had been so devastated. The mists of November were wrapping themselves around us by the time we returned to the homestead. There we prepared to celebrate Christmas.

"Father, what usually happens here at Yuletide?" I asked Ealdwine.

"We aren't often here," the priest admitted. "Christmas is a time when the court often meets and takes the opportunity to do business, so all the aethelings and thegns are with the King – wherever he happens to be."

"But not this year?"

Ealdwine shook his head.

"As you know, things are not good between the King and our lord," he conceded. "It is very painful to be ignored or denigrated, so our lord has chosen to stay here."

"Will you take the service?" I asked.

"No, there is a local priest who'll do that. We'll join with the other villagers."

So on Christmas Eve, late in the night, we set out from the homestead with blazing torches and picked our way through the darkness to the church. Here we stood outside while the priest read from the bible. It was all in Latin, but I recognised some words and thought it must be the beginning of St. John's Gospel. I remembered that from our time in the monastery at Evesham.

Around midnight we were allowed into the church, the

entrance to which had been decked with branches of yew and holly. We took in the light and proclaimed how the Light of the World had come when Christ was born.

The priest preached a homily on how Jesus can change things – people and events – and how he brings a message of hope to a dark and sinful world. Then he said the Mass and we all received bread and wine, those living symbols of Christ's body and blood, a reminder of his humanity, a pointer to his divinity.

We came out of the church to find the land was white. The gently falling snow sizzled on our torches but could not put them out.

Later in the day, we feasted well, including wild boar. The hall was warm, a bright fire in the centre, and we filled it with laughter and riddles.

"Wulfgar," Aelfnoth challenged, "do you know this one?

'I travel by foot, trample the ground,
the green fields, for as long as I live.
Lifeless, I fetter dark Welshmen,
sometimes their betters too. At times
I give a warrior liquor from within me,
at times a stately bride steps on me;
sometimes a slave-girl, raven-haired,
brought far from Wales, cradles and presses me –
some stupid, sozzled maidservant, she fills me
with water on dark nights, warms me
by the gleaming fire; on my breast

she places a wanton hand and writhes about,
then sweeps me against her dark declivity.
What am I called who, alive, lay waste
the land and, dead, serve humankind?'"

"Sounds like a piss pot," chortled one man.

"I wouldn't drink from that!" responded another.

"It does sound like a bottle, or at least something that holds liquid," I conceded.

"But in the riddle it was also alive," Aelfnoth reminded me and he repeated the words.

Some lewd conversation carried on around me, while I struggled to think what it could be.

"It is something that's alive, but when it's dead, it's used for holding liquid," I mused. "Oh, I have it! It's leather. It's the cow in the field whose coat is tanned and we use the leather for shoes and for vessels."

"Clever lad!"

I glowed.

We stayed at the homestead for the worst of the weather, then we were on the move again, this time south into Kent along its coast and into Sussex.

The pattern from the previous autumn was repeated with my lord staying briefly with a thegn, but discussing at length the coastal defences in the area.

I think it was somewhere near Chichester where I first met lord Godwine. His estate was at Compton and he welcomed us warmly.

"My lord Edmund, I am your servant," he declared.

"You served my brother well," my lord responded.

"And he was gracious to me in death," our host added.

Later, as we enjoyed his hospitality, Aelfnoth told me what he knew.

"Wulfgar, do you remember I told you about the mess up with the ships?"

"When so many were lost because of a feud?" I answered.

"Yes. The feud was between Wulfnoth and Brihtric."

"One of them was earl Eadric's brother," I recalled.

"That was Brihtric. But the other man, Wulfnoth, who was accused, unjustly, by Brihtric was lord Godwine's father."

I looked across the hall at the well-built thegn chatting easily to my lord. I guessed he was in his late twenties.

"Wulfnoth fled abroad after he burned Brihtric's fleet," Aelfnoth continued, "and the King confiscated his lands and gave them to lord Athelstan. He held them for six years, but in his will he returned them to Wulfnoth's family. In fact, he allowed lord Godwine to manage them even before he died."

We continued along the south coast as far as Dorset, then we turned north and spent a few days near Bath. We seemed to be avoiding the large towns and I commented on this to Ealdwine.

"I think our lord is doing what I suggested," the priest replied. "He is building relationships with as many thegns and estate-holders as he can. He is soothing troubled feathers – many are still feeling raw from the King's failure last year."

"Bath was one of the places Swein captured, wasn't it?" I asked.

"Yes and people from all across this area went there to submit," Ealdwine remembered. "Even earl Aethelmaer came out of his monastery. I expect our lord will pay him a visit when we are in the area of Eynsham."

Our journey north brought us to Deerhurst and the home of Odda, his young wife and their two children. The estate bordered the great river Severn on its western side. The melting snow of winter had brought the level of the water close to flooding the meadows, but the homestead was built on slightly higher ground and so was safe. There was also a huge church there, on the north side of which an angel claimed God's protection for the building.

"This is a homely, happy household," I remarked to Ealdwine. "They have made us very welcome."

"There is something intangible here," he acknowledged. "A peace. It's a place that gives balm to the soul. Perhaps it is all the prayer, for this must have been a holy site for many years."

Even my lord seemed reluctant to move on, but move on we did; we followed the river north through the land of the Hwicce. We celebrated Easter in Worcester and met again Archbishop Wulfstan. I wasn't privy to my lord's conversation with him this time, but they seemed at ease with each other and we were made welcome in the city.

After Easter, we crossed the Severn by the bridge at Worcester and headed north-west. On our travels we came near again to the Severn.

"This must be a very long river," I commented to Aelfnoth.

"Ah, yes, it rises in Wales, beyond our land," he told me. "You see it here, where it can be forded with care. Then it flows north to Shrewsbury before going south through Worcester and then Deerhurst, by which time it's a great river and you need a boat to get across."

"Are we going to Shrewsbury?" I wondered.

"I doubt it," he muttered. "Earl Eadric's stronghold." He raised his eyebrows. "Not a place we'd be too welcome I guess."

He was right, for we soon turned east and crossed the Severn by a bridge near a burgh established by King Alfred's daughter – or so I was told. I think it was called Bridgnorth.

"We're heading home now, Wulfgar," Ealdwine confided. "My lord should be pleased with the work he's done these last few months. I think there's been much healing."

I smiled. I too was pleased to see how well lord Edmund had been received in so many homesteads. Back home the shearing should have been in full swing and I would soon be busy counting fleeces and sending some to market.

It was nearly a year since lord Athelstan's death and I

was sure my lord still felt it – the loss of a brother, the possibility of his becoming king, but in that year I reckoned he had changed, he had become more serious.

Maybe this summer will be a quiet one, I thought.

How wrong I was!

CHAPTER 15

"Wulfgar, I want you to go to Oxford."

"Yes, my lord."

I wiped the sweat from my brow.

"You'll go with Aelfnoth." My lord looked across at me and I paused in my work of recording fleeces sent to market. "My father's called a meeting of the Witan there."

"Will you not go yourself?" I asked.

"I haven't been invited." He shrugged his shoulders. "I'm not sure why. Perhaps something is going on that he doesn't want me to know about. That's why I'm sending you, for you have a way of picking up news without people noticing you are there."

I couldn't help but grin. He was right. I saw it as a talent I had and one I could use well for my lord.

"Couldn't you go anyway?" I suggested.

"I could, but there's no point making things any worse between us," he admitted. "Athelstan could do no wrong, but I have to tread a more careful path."

I thought I understood, but it wasn't my place to argue anyway.

"Folk will associate Aelfnoth with Athelstan, so they won't see him as my spy. At least, I don't think they will. His job really will be as your travelling companion. If there's any spying to be done, that's your job."

I rather liked the idea of being a spy. I knew the

actual meeting of the Witan would not be open to me, but I could listen to the gossip of the retainers.

The journey wasn't pleasant in the heat of late July, but at least it wasn't raining. As we passed through the countryside, we could see that much of the harvest had been gathered in and soon we would celebrate the first loaf at Lammas. There should be plenty of food for the gathering in Oxford.

Aelfnoth found us a place to bed down and a stable for our horses. I hadn't been to Oxford before and thought it looked a wealthy place, for there were many new buildings.

"A lot of damage was done in the time of Swein," Aelfnoth told me. "The town is looking a lot smarter than when I was last here." Then he added with a knowing wink, "This is one of earl Eadric's towns."

"He's put money into it?"

"Yes. His heartland is Shrewsbury, but he's managed to extend his influence beyond the land of the Magonsaete and into the land of the Hwicce."

"I thought earl Leofwine headed up the Hwicce."

"He's not the head now – it's earl Eadric – all do his bidding," he confided. "In fact, here we are really beyond even the land of the Hwicce, so you can see how far his power reaches."

"Do you think earl Eadric will be in charge?"

"Oh yes, he's the King's man through and through and the King will have asked him to organise this gathering."

"But why Oxford and not London, as usual?" I queried.

"I don't know, for even the earls from the farthest reaches of the kingdom are often found with the King in London. You're here to find out, aren't you?"

He grinned and I grinned back.

"I'm off to find an old friend. Go and do some snooping," he laughed.

So I did. There was the usual great hall, a large timber-framed structure with a thatched roof and here the King and his retinue would be eating. The King himself had a separate place where he would sleep, guarded by his men. The many thegns who had been called to the Witan would also have found somewhere to lodge and each would have brought some of their household with them.

I wondered how I could infiltrate the gathering and decided the kitchen might be a good place to start. Huge quantities of food would be necessary for all these people who would probably feast together in the hall.

I followed my nose and soon found the building where the cooking was being done.

"Want any help?" I enquired.

A red-faced man, dripping sweat, and who didn't look as though he ever smiled, grunted and waved me away.

"I'm good at kneading bread," I offered.

He fixed me with his eye and looked me up and down. I was obviously no beggar off the street. I'm sure he could tell by my clothes that I served a rich man.

141

"You know how to knead?" he growled.

"Yes. You must be having to bake a lot of extra bread."

"We are." He paused. "Alright, but wash your grubby hands first."

I obeyed and then got stuck in to my task. I thought he might ask me awkward questions, but he was too busy. One of the other workers did ask me who I served.

"I'm here with Aelfnoth, but he's gone off to find someone and told me to make myself useful to someone else."

It wasn't quite true, but it was enough, and once they saw how hard I worked, they made no further enquiry and I could listen. Not that they seemed to know much, for all that concerned them was not burning the roasting meat and making sure there was enough food for all the guests.

"Does your master want you back?" the head cook asked.

"Not till tonight," I answered. "Do you want help with the carrying and serving?"

"Yes."

So I got to carry food into the great hall and see who had gathered.

Everyone was busy eating and talking, so I felt sure no one was looking at me. Anyway, the last time I had seen some of these men was over a year ago in York when we celebrated Easter and I had grown since then. So I moved quietly from table to table with the plates of meat, vegetables and bread, and while I moved, I made a mental note of the faces I recognised.

Among them was earl Leofwine, but even he didn't seem to recognise me. Earl Ulfketel and earl Uhtred were there with the ladies I took to be their wives, the King's daughters. I also spotted earl Morcar and earl Siferth, the latter having his pretty wife with him. The earl of Mercia, of course, was presiding over the whole as a host though deferring constantly to the King.

What a creep! I thought, but made sure I had no eye contact with him, though I doubted he'd remember me.

There were many other well-dressed men there whom I took to be thegns, but there were none I could put a name to.

So, who was *not* there? The Queen for a start, which I did wonder at, and also her children. Perhaps they were all in London, though many thegns appeared to have brought their wives. Earl Eadric had no woman with him, but I had never seen his wife, so I was assuming she was not elsewhere in the hall. Also missing was the aetheling Eadwig, as well as his older brother, my lord.

As I lay on my pallet gazing at the thatch and wondering where Aelfnoth was, I went over in my head the information I'd gathered. Earl Eadric and the King were most definitely in charge, but there were people not present whom I thought would be there. Perhaps my lord would make more sense of it when I returned.

Aelfnoth came to his bed after I had fallen asleep and he was drunk enough to wake me with his clumsiness.

"Had a good time?" I mumbled.

"Oh, yes, she was just as good as the last time." He hiccupped as he flopped on the pallet. He didn't bother with the blanket, but then neither had I, for the night was sultry.

The next day the Witan met, so all the retainers were abroad in Oxford with nothing much to do, while their masters debated matters of state.

They're probably raising taxes, I thought. Or arguing about raising taxes. The King will do what he likes.

He had promised to be a more gracious monarch and to rule more justly when he returned from exile, but I hadn't seen much evidence of that and comments my lord had let slip suggested he was sceptical about his father's 'change of heart'.

I was deep in such thoughts when someone grabbed my arm and pulled me into the shadows.

"You are lord Edmund's boy!"

My face was inches away from that of the lady Frida and I felt it go very hot.

"Yes," I spluttered.

"Is he here?" she demanded.

"No, my lady."

"Why not?"

What should I say? The truth?

"He wasn't invited," I muttered.

She frowned and I hated to see her pretty face look so worried.

"That's very strange. But you're here!"

I gulped. She was still holding my arm tightly, so I couldn't run away.

"My lord wants to know what happens," I admitted.

She nodded, her face relaxed and she let me go.

"He is well?"

"Yes, my lady."

"Busy?"

"Yes, he's been visiting the coast and inspecting our defences." I paused. Should I have said that?

"He will make a fine king," and she flashed me a beautiful smile before she moved quickly away and left my face to cool. I scolded myself for blushing and stayed in the shade until I thought she had walked some distance.

I wondered about returning to the kitchen, for the work was hot and hard, but it did give me an excuse to go into the hall and generally be around the thegns. No one noticed a lad carrying plates, well, one person had and I was surprised, for I hadn't noticed the lady Frida's eyes ever turning in my direction. She obviously had a gift of noticing others without being noticed herself – and that thought made me smile – and blush again!

I went back to the kitchen and fitted in like a hand in a personally made glove. I became part of the furniture, which was exactly what I needed.

The King and his thegns feasted well again that

evening and the mead was flowing. I observed earl Siferth was very merry and even earl Morcar had the occasional smile. Perhaps it had been a good meeting of the Witan. I hadn't managed to get any information on what had been discussed, but, from the atmosphere in the hall, I guessed the thegns were happy. The King too was smiling, as was earl Eadric.

The meal was almost over and I was removing some of the empty platters when I saw the earl of Mercia speaking to earl Morcar and earl Siferth and the three of them left the hall, together with a couple of other men I guessed were thegns but didn't know. They were slapping each other's backs and enjoying a joke. I thought nothing of it.

Aelfnoth was asleep and snoring when I got to bed, but despite the heat and the noise he made, I was soon asleep. I had promised the cook I would help with the clearing up of the hall in the morning.

When I did get into the hall, there was still debris from the feast the previous evening, but also quite a number of people. I was surprised to see the King was sitting there, with several of his thegns around him, apparently deep in conversation. There were other men in groups in other parts of the hall and as I moved among the tables, I began to sense something was wrong. I didn't have long to wait to find out if my suspicions were well-founded.

There was a commotion at the door and the lady Frida appeared. She screamed so loudly that everyone froze where they were. I couldn't take my eyes off her. She pulled her gown free of her feet and ran to where the King sat. There she fell on her knees.

"My lord!" she cried through her tears. "My husband has been murdered!"

CHAPTER 16

The King flinched slightly, but his face showed no emotion.

"My lord!" the lady Frida cried again. "Earl Eadric has killed my husband and earl Morcar!"

No one in the hall moved; we were all gripped by this drama of an aggrieved wife.

"I demand justice!" she wailed.

"You have received it," was the cold response. "Your husband and his brother were traitors and have been punished accordingly."

People gasped, including me.

"No, my lord!" she screamed. "They were your loyal servants."

"They swore allegiance to a foreigner and have now paid the price for their treachery." The King almost spat out these words.

He turned to two of his retainers.

"Bind this woman," he ordered. "She too is a traitor. Take her to the abbey at Malmesbury and tell the abbot to lock her up."

The lady Frida screamed again – the sound pierced our souls. But it was to no avail. She was surrounded by the King's men and dragged from the great hall. For a moment, no one spoke and then suddenly everyone was talking and I realised for the first time that the earl of Mercia was missing.

I abandoned the plates and ran looking for Aelfnoth. He had news too, which he shared, after I had panted out an account of the scene in the hall.

"It's true," he confirmed. "Earl Eadric had Morcar and Siferth killed last night."

"I saw them all leave the hall, but there were others too."

"Just a blind. Eadric somehow got Morcar and Siferth alone in his house and his men set upon them. They didn't stand a chance."

"But surely they weren't traitors as the King says?"

"They submitted to Swein and now they've paid the price."

"But others submitted too," I argued.

"Earl Ulfketel and earl Uhtred are married to his daughters and so he can't 'dispose' of them as such and he killed the earl of Lindsey last year. No, I'm afraid Morcar and Siferth had no defence, no guardian after my lord had died. They were vulnerable."

The horror of what had happened was beginning to sink in.

"That's why our lord's not here," Aelfnoth added quietly. "I doubt the King would have allowed this if our lord Edmund had been here. He would have led an outcry. As it is, he wasn't here and now they're dead and earl Siferth's widow's a prisoner at the King's pleasure." He paused. "And you know what else that means?"

"There's something more?" I gasped.

"The King will seize their holdings in the Five Boroughs," he grunted. "And then either keep them to increase his wealth or give them to some favourite."

"Like the man who does his dirty work for him," I responded, knowing Aelfnoth knew who I meant.

"We need to take this news to our lord."

"But we don't yet know what the Witan talked about," I argued.

"What the Witan talked about is irrelevant," was the sardonic response. "We know the meeting was held and why it was held in Oxford – it was all about revenge. And the King's got it now."

So we left and returned home in haste.

My lord looked stunned at the news, his face so frozen I couldn't read his expression. I felt the world had stopped – but not for long. He leapt up and shouted orders.

"We ride to Malmesbury – now! Ealdwine, I'll need you."

I thought he might have left me behind, so was pleased to find I was included, but I dared not ask why we should go to Malmesbury. Did my lord really want to express his condolences to earl Siferth's widow in person? He could surely send a messenger. I said nothing though.

Two days of travelling brought us to Wiltshire and the town of Malmesbury. It was late afternoon when we arrived at the gates of the Abbey.

"Open in the name of the King!" my lord shouted.

The porter was reluctant to obey until my lord

produced his seal. Then he grunted and opened the small door in the huge gate. We all dismounted.

"Ealdwine, Wulfgar, come with me. The rest of you wait here."

So we three ducked into the interior. Here my lord removed his sword and gave it to me to carry.

"I come in peace," he told the porter. "I wish to see the abbot."

The porter hesitated and then waved in the direction of a door off the courtyard.

"My lord, you can wait in here while I fetch him."

The room was small but set with chairs and appeared to be a place where visitors could be received without their impinging on the life of the Abbey.

Several minutes passed with my lord pacing back and forth, while Ealdwine and I sat more patiently. I guessed neither of us knew quite why we were there. Then the door opened and an elderly man entered.

"Father," my lord began, "I'm sorry to interrupt your life of prayer, but I ... I come from the King regarding the lady Frida."

The abbot inclined his head slightly to one side.

"The lady Frida only arrived here recently," he began, "and I have the King's orders to ... to detain her."

"The King has reconsidered. Placing her here was a temporary measure. It is an inappropriate place for her – long term."

"I agree, a nunnery would be more suitable," the cleric responded.

"She is to be released into my custody."

I nearly dropped the sword! My lord was rebelling against his father! I hadn't expected that.

The abbot had his eyes fixed on his face, but my lord didn't flinch. He was brazen in his lying!

"Do you have his letter of authority?" he asked.

"I am the King's son. I think we have met at court, but some years ago. Here is my seal. Ealdwine is my chaplain and he can vouch for my identity."

Still he hesitated.

"Indeed, Father, I can vouch for him," Ealdwine interposed. "I have been chaplain to my lord Edmund for several years. Surely he would not come on such a mission unless he had been sent by the King?"

I wanted to clap Ealdwine as he knew as well as I that the King had *not* sent his son on this mission.

"I will fetch the lady Frida, but you are not to speak to her until I say you can."

My lord did not catch our eyes while we waited. He continued to pace the small room. Then the abbot returned with the lady Frida. No blue gown today – she was dressed in black and her eyes were downcast.

"My lady, these men say they are from the King and ask that I release you to them," the abbot said. "Do you know them?"

The lady Frida lifted her eyes and I saw her frown slightly.

"Yes," she replied quietly, "I do know these men. This is the aetheling, my lord Edmund, and his chaplain."

"You are happy to go with them to the King?"

"I am happy to go with them."

The abbot now turned to my lord.

"I have your word you will take her to the King?" he asked.

The movement of his head could have been interpreted as assent.

"I am taking her north," he answered. "My lady Frida, you have personal items you brought with you here?"

"A few."

"While the lady Frida prepares for her journey, I'll have some refreshments sent in for you," the abbot informed us and he swept out, taking his prisoner with him.

We still said nothing. Some ale and bread arrived soon afterwards and we all ate in silence, though I noticed my lord was pulling his bread into pieces but putting little in his mouth.

Ealdwine wrapped some of the bread in a cloth and put it within his gown. He caught me watching him.

"For the journey north," he said, almost smiling.

I was glad when the lady Frida was delivered to my lord and we were free to leave, as I had an uneasy feeling about our mission and was puzzled that my lord should be opposing his father's commands. Thus the sound of the small door shutting behind us and the sight of our horses was a relief.

Once outside the abbey compound, I thought we would mount and ride away at speed, but my lord grasped the lady Frida and kissed her so hungrily that I thought he hurt her. Indeed I feared he would ravish her there and then, but when he let her go, I saw her face and she was shining, bright with desire for him, more than enough to match his own. Then I understood why we had come.

CHAPTER 17

The next day they married and Ealdwine gave them God's blessing.

My lord despatched two of our party to return to our homestead with a message, but he kept me in the group that travelled north. We kept well away from Oxford, and after a few days reached earl Siferth's home in Derbyshire.

The household there was in a state of shock, for those who had been in Oxford had returned with the news of their lord's murder and his wife's imprisonment and they didn't know what to do. Now, suddenly, their lady was in their midst again and they wanted to rejoice at that, but grieve with her for the loss of her husband. My lord called them all together.

"You have heard what happened in Oxford," he began, "how your lord was despicably murdered on the orders of earl Eadric of Mercia. He lured him and his brother, earl Morcar, into his house and had them killed."

He looked around at the forlorn faces.

"I have to tell you, it is worse than that, if that be possible. My father ..." He looked down and fidgeted with his belt. "My father was complicit in this murder."

Some gasped, but I think others had already guessed.

"I am ashamed of his action," my lord continued. "Your lord and his brother did indeed submit to Swein, but they returned to the King and have been his loyal thegns since the King returned from exile. I believed they had been forgiven and had received mercy from the King."

Again he fiddled with his belt and found it difficult to meet their eyes.

"I was wrong," he admitted, with great sadness in his voice. "It seems my father has simply been waiting for an opportunity to take vengeance and he has now done that. He ... he pretended friendship, but was really their enemy."

They were all listening intently. The hall was so quiet that I could hear some birds singing outside.

"Not only did the King ensure the death of your lord, but he compounded his actions by the unjust imprisonment of your lady. She was taken to Malmesbury and would still be there if I had not rescued her. The King, of course, plans to seize your lord's holdings and that of his brother."

"Shame on him," muttered one man.

My lord looked across at him.

"Yes, shame on him," he agreed. "He will have to face judgment before Almighty God for his actions."

He now glanced at the lady Frida, who had been standing nearby while he spoke.

"Your lady needed a protector," he informed them and stretched out his hand, into which she slipped hers. "I have married her and I pray you will now accept me as your lord."

For a moment, they all looked completely stunned. This wasn't what they'd expected. Then one man knelt, and another, and then all of them.

"You are our lord," they said, and my lord smiled his thanks, and his lady smiled too.

Before we lost the light on that momentous day in late August, I saw my lord and his lady walk to the nearby church and hover in its graveyard. I guessed earl Siferth's retainers had brought his body home and had him buried. I saw the lady Frida bend down and place what looked like flowers on the heap of soil and I said a quiet prayer for the repose of her late husband's soul. Then she turned and fell to weeping in my lord's arms and I turned away, for I felt I shouldn't be watching them.

We spent only a few days there, and whilst there was a sense of sadness over the death of earl Siferth, there was a palpable sense of relief that their lady was safe and they had a new lord, one they could respect. No one spoke ill of my lord Edmund, or if they did, it wasn't in my hearing, but I believe they were happy to have him, for they thought him a man of integrity.

Aelfnoth had joined us and he was shocked at what had happened.

"He's in rebellion against the King," he whispered to me.

I think I knew that!

"All for some land," he added. "I hope it's worth it."

"It's not just the land," I countered. "There is the lady, remember."

"Oh, people will say he's married her for the land, so he can be lord of the Five Boroughs."

"But you know better!"

"Do I?" He sounded sceptical.

"He's in love with her."

He raised his eyebrows.

"Are you sure?"

For a moment I hesitated. Then I saw their faces again outside Malmesbury Abbey.

"Yes, I'm sure," I asserted. "Remember I was there when he rescued her and I saw them. And I have seen them since. I don't doubt his love for her."

Aelfnoth grunted.

"Tis a good job then that she is pretty and brings to the marriage much land."

I could see he wouldn't be convinced immediately. I could look back to the first time I had seen them together and I realised now that a flame burned then, though low. A year later he had greatly feared she'd been defiled by the Danes and was relieved she'd been left unharmed. The fire had been there, but they had each contained it until earl Siferth's death left them free to let it burn. And now it burned hotly, for I lay outside my lord's room and I could hear them in the night, their laughter and their gasps of pleasure. She was a very willing wife.

My lord assembled his retainers and told us we were moving on, the Derbyshire homestead being left in the capable hands of the seneschal. We moved from place to place so that my lord could receive the homage of those on his new holdings. He took the lady Frida with him, partly

I think to convince the tenants that he was the genuine successor to the brother earls and partly because he couldn't bear to be parted from her – or she from him.

So we travelled the areas of Derby, Nottingham and Leicester and came to Stamford where we celebrated the Feast of the Nativity of the Blessed Virgin Mary. Everywhere the people submitted to my lord, accepting him with relief, glad he had not allowed the King to seize the land.

"Father Ealdwine, I'm surprised it's been so easy," I commented to the priest. "Surely the King must be very angry."

"I expect he is, but what can he do?"

I shrugged my shoulders.

"Is it likely, Wulfgar, that he will bring an army against his own son?"

"He ... he might," I answered.

"Yes, he might, but I think he won't. The King has no iron grip on this area," he went on. "There are no royal holdings, nor are there any great abbeys under the control of the King. Without lands and monasteries up here, the King has not been able to reinforce his authority by regular visits such as he does in Wessex and Mercia. He has relied on local men."

"So ... so why have the earls killed, for they were loyal to him?"

Ealdwine sighed.

"I don't know," he admitted. "They did submit to

Swein, but turned back to the King. He must have taken their submission to a foreigner deeply to heart and never forgiven them."

"But, surely, he should have?"

"Yes, Wulfgar, they repented and appeared to be forgiven. What was done at Oxford was very wrong and the King condoned it, even if he did not authorise it. And now he has paid a heavy price." He looked at me. "The King has lost these lands *and* lost his son," he said quietly, "and that weakens our country, for the Danes will pounce on a divided nation."

"You think they'll be back?"

"Oh, yes, I don't doubt that. Cnut will have licked his wounds by now. But here we are talking of great matters when we have work to do."

Ealdwine had taken over as my teacher and would sometimes have me write letters for him.

"Lord Edmund has asked me to prepare two diplomas and you can help me," he explained. "They are grants of land held by earl Siferth. The one is of land at Peakirk and Walton in the shire of Northampton, which is to be given to the New Minster in Winchester for the souls of our lord, his wife and the late earl. The other is of land at Lakenheath in Suffolk, which is to be given to the Abbey at Thorney for the security of our lord and his lady."

"I don't remember you doing this kind of work before," I commented.

Ealdwine did not answer immediately.

160

"You're right," he said at length. "Diplomas such as these are only issued by kings."

I felt the hairs rise on my arms.

"Is our lord ...?"

I couldn't finish.

"It is a bold action," was the priest's response. "Let us hope it is not a foolhardy one," he quietly added.

Once all of the men who previously acknowledged earl Morcar and earl Siferth as their lords had accepted my lord Edmund, we returned to the homestead in Derbyshire. There had been no word from the King, but none of us doubted he knew what had happened. There was, however, some news which might have explained the King's silence. We got to hear that the King had been taken ill while still in Oxford and had remained there as a guest of earl Eadric until he was recovered. In that short time, my lord had been able to seize the initiative and now, really, it was too late for the King to come north in an attempt to bring his errant son to heel, for the whole area was my lord's.

I will not say we were complacent, but we were in a relaxed mood, for we heard the King had now gone south, perhaps to Winchester, and thus there would be no confrontation. The warmth of late September and the burnished colours of the trees gave a homely glow to the group of buildings and there was music in the hall each evening and the sound of laughter.

Our peace was soon shattered.

CHAPTER 18

By the time it reached us, the news was several days old and therefore it wasn't clear what my lord Edmund should do. He did, however, despatch messengers north to check on the Humber and the Trent and also east to see what could be learned from those living in East Anglia and especially on the coast. While he waited, he sent out a call to raise the local fyrd.

The news that had disturbed our peace was that Danish ships had been sighted off the Kent coast. Two years earlier Swein had brought his fleet into the Humber and up the Trent, but there was a different situation here now. Swein may have reckoned on being welcomed or at least finding thegns disgruntled with their King and willing to renege. Now, if Cnut had spies here, he would know the area was united against the Danes. There was earl Uhtred to the north and earl Ulfketel in the east and the Five Boroughs loyal to my lord. York itself had been a nestbed of opposition to the King, but was happy to support his rebellious son.

The weakness of the nation was our disunity, but my lord now sought to address this.

"Wulfgar, prepare parchment and ink," Ealdwine ordered, "for I have to write a letter to the earl of Mercia."

"Really?"

I set about my task, but was astonished that my lord should correspond with his wife's enemy.

"My lord realises that we need to fight the Danes, not each other," Ealdwine explained. "He's right, of course, and I hope earl Eadric agrees with him."

I wasn't very hopeful. My last sighting of earl Eadric was of him smiling an invitation to earls Morcar and Siferth and leading them out to their deaths. He would know my lord had now married the lady Frida, so he would hardly be expecting an olive branch.

I was therefore somewhat surprised when told several days later to prepare for a journey. Our party included Ealdwine and just enough men to protect my lord.

"Wulfgar, we are going to Tamworth," my lord declared as we set off. "What do you know about that place?"

"Nothing, my lord," I confessed.

"Tut, tut," he chided, with a smile. "Tamworth is close to the great Roman road called Watling Street, which used to divide our country in the time of the great King Alfred. Before his time, it was the capital of the ancient kingdom of Mercia."

"So it was a kingdom once?"

"Yes, along with Wessex and Northumbria," he explained. "They were the great kingdoms and there were smaller areas where a bretwald, or under-king, ruled. So you've never heard of King Offa?"

"Only that you've got a sword of his," I answered.

"Is that *all* you know?"

"Yes," I conceded, feeling my ignorance.

"Tamworth was his home and he ruled Mercia from there, oh, more than two hundred years ago. He caused a great dyke to be made between the English and the Welsh."

"So people can't cross?"

"It can be crossed. It's no huge barrier. Really it marks out the land, it makes clear what is England and what is Wales and thus all know when they have crossed the boundary. It hasn't stopped the perennial raiding that happens."

"I've heard the Welsh are wild."

He laughed.

"No more wild than us, Wulfgar. They have some different ways, but they are men as we are. The English are as prone to steal another's cattle as the Welsh are."

I'd never met a Welshman, so I took his word for it. In my head I had noted that Tamworth was in Mercia, so earl Eadric had not been asked to come into the Five Boroughs, but neither were we going right over to Shrewsbury where I understood he had his main home. We would be meeting him on the border between my lord's territory and his.

Tamworth might have been a 'capital' once, but now it was like many other towns, a jumble of buildings, a busy market and people trying to make money. We picked our way through the crowds to a timber-framed hall, the home, I guessed, of a local thegn.

"My lord Edmund," a grey-haired man greeted us, "I

164

am honoured to have you as my guest."

We saw other horses there to which a groom was attending.

"Earl Eadric is already here?" my lord enquired.

"He is," our host replied. "I have some refreshment for you all."

The meal was somewhat tense. Earl Eadric had little to say, while my lord endeavoured to make conversation with the thegn and his wife by enquiring after his family, how the harvest had been and preparations for the winter.

"We are hoping for a winter free of strife," the thegn acknowledged.

"We hope for that too," my lord assured him, "but the matter of peace is not entirely in our hands."

He had glanced at the earl of Mercia, but he was concentrating on pulling some meat from a bone and would not catch his eye.

Eventually, the two parties who had come to talk were left to get on with it. Ealdwine stayed close to my lord and earl Eadric too had a chaplain, a wraith of a man with no flesh on him and a sour expression. I was told to sit by the door and look after my lord's sword. Neither of them was meant to have a weapon.

"What news have you?" my lord asked. "I cannot find that the Danes have sailed north."

"What I've heard is that Cnut's in charge and he's taken his fleet along the south coast," the earl responded.

"So this is serious – if Cnut's here."

"He may have come back simply to steal."

"But it's more likely he has a taste for conquest," my lord suggested.

Earl Eadric was quiet.

"Where's the King?"

"Your father was heading for Winchester with the intention of securing the area."

"So he is recovered?"

"For the moment." The earl paused. "His health has not been good these last two years and the bouts of sickness are increasing in frequency."

My lord sighed. If something happened to the King, he was the aetheling most likely to succeed to the throne and from what I'd seen that summer he was already acting like a king in waiting. Even if he was thinking this, he said nothing to the earl and I thought it unlikely the earl would know about the diplomas. Neither of them had made any mention of earl Siferth and the lady Frida and I didn't think they would!

"And Thorkell?" my lord asked.

"He's with his ships in London unless by now he's received orders to harry the Danish fleet."

"For the moment then Mercia and the north are not threatened," my lord concluded. "Wessex is the place in danger. We could take a combined force south to aid the King."

"I cannot spare men," the earl suddenly objected. "I need them to guard the western boundary."

"What?! Cnut comes here to conquer us and you won't help?!" My lord was clearly shocked.

"The Welsh are troublesome," the earl complained.

"I've met the leaders in Powys and they have given me their word they won't take advantage of us while we're threatened by the Danes," my lord assured him.

Now it was the earl's turn to be shocked.

"You've met the Welsh?" His tone was incredulous and sarcastic. "You've done some kind of deal with them?!"

"No deal. We simply spoke man to man about the danger posed by the Danes and both agreed we didn't want England to be conquered. I believe they'll stick to their word and there'll be no border trouble for the time being."

Earl Eadric stood up.

"I'll have no dealings with a man who has talked to the Welsh," he declared, and stormed out of the hall, with his chaplain hurrying to keep up with him.

My lord also stood and called after the earl, "For the sake of England!"

I wondered if he would run after him, but Ealdwine laid a gentle hand on his arm.

"You did your best, my lord," he said. "I fear he never meant to give you aid. And now he will go home feeling justified in his refusal."

"So, have I made things worse?"

"You offered reconciliation and that was your

Christian duty," his chaplain assured him. "Under God, you did what was right." He sighed. "I fear there is some demon in the earl's heart that means he cannot receive your outstretched hand. Though he cannot fight with you, let's pray he does not fight against you."

I felt desperately sorry for my lord. He had set up this meeting and had had to face the man who'd killed his wife's husband. He'd had to put such matters to one side in order to eat with him and then speak with him. The earl had just about been polite, but he seemed to have made no effort at compromise. Perhaps he had always intended to go off in a huff, and the Welsh were his excuse for doing so. I felt my lord had been slapped in the face.

"I suppose he does have a problem with the Welsh," my lord admitted.

"If so, it is of his own making," Ealdwine countered. "Did he not lead a campaign into the south, even as far as St. David's, wreaking havoc?"

"That must be three years ago though."

"The Welsh are not likely to forget, my lord. If there is trouble on the border, some of it is of the earl's own making. Come. We have done what we could. Let's return and you can find comfort with your lady."

I'm sure the lady Frida did comfort my lord, for once back in her arms, his spirits did rise.

On my own one day with Ealdwine, I took the opportunity to ask him about the Welsh.

"I've served my lord Edmund for nearly two years," I

began, "and I've never heard he met the Welsh. When did that happen?"

"I've been wondering about that myself," he confessed. "I've been with him many years and to my knowledge he has never met the leaders of Powys. But ..." He gave me a sly glance and lowered his voice. "Do you remember last autumn? When we went into Shropshire?"

I nodded.

"My lord went on a hunting trip and he didn't take you or me with him, or indeed any of his retainers, just two local men."

Something was stirring in my memory.

"He said I might get in the way," I responded. "It could be dangerous, with arrows or spears flying through the air."

"And certainly a hunting trip is no place for an elderly priest," Ealdwine added.

"But they brought something back," I countered, "for surely we ate roasted meat that night?"

"Maybe they caught it – or maybe they were given it as part of their meeting with the Welsh," Ealdwine suggested. "We were very close to the border there, near the ford over the Severn called Rhyd-y-Groes. Men from each country could easily have met there."

It all made sense now. My lord had used a visit to a friendly homestead to cover up his meeting with some Welsh leaders. None of us had guessed, and his two companions had kept his secret well.

I was angry inside. If earl Eadric had crossed my path at that moment, I would have thumped him – except I only came up to his chest and he would have crushed me with a single blow. My lord was trying so hard to save us from the Danes, and the earl of Mercia wasn't helping. I didn't think it could get any worse, but there I was wrong.

CHAPTER 19

Following his meeting with earl Eadric, my lord had disbanded the fyrd and sent the men home. There was no fighting in our area and no way he could take a force south through Mercia to aid the King. He did, however, continue to send men to seek news.

The first information related to Cnut and the Danish fleet. They had continued along the south coast and from what we heard, it sounded as though they hadn't been challenged and so had been able to shelter in the great harbour at Poole.

"Why hasn't Thorkell been ordered to fight them?" my lord demanded, but no one had an answer. "What is my father doing? Why doesn't he raise a force? He's down there somewhere."

He was pacing up and down the hall and fiddling with his belt.

"Do you want to go south and find out?" my lady asked.

She was sitting near the fire, for a chill October wind was finding its way through every crack. My lord went over to her and took her hand in his.

"I don't want to leave you," he said softly.

He rubbed her hand.

"You are cold, my love," he complained. "Are you sick?"

She had a smile to set any man's heart racing and she

gave him one now.

"No, I'm well, my lord. Just a little chilled."

"Some broth for my lady," he ordered and a servant ran to oblige. "I will stay, but I wish the news were better."

It was nearing All Hallows when we received more news.

"News from Winchester, my lord!" A rider swathed in a warm cloak hurried in disturbing our meal.

"Yes?" My lord leapt up.

"The King is ill. He lies sick at Cosham."

"God preserve him!" cried his son and he sank back into his chair.

"He was in Southampton, raising forces to secure Hampshire when he fell ill," the messenger continued.

"And the Danes? Where are they?" my lord asked, leaning forward and gripping the arms of the chair.

"Still in Dorset, it's believed."

"In the harbour?"

"No, they've been leaving their ships and raiding inland," the messenger answered. "They've attacked villages in Dorset and Wiltshire and, some say, even in Somerset."

"And does no one seek to stop them?"

The messenger slowly shook his head.

"None, my lord."

"Come, rest and eat. You've had a hard journey," my lady said. "We are grateful for your news, though what we hear does not cheer us."

My lord remained distracted and deep in thought, not just for that day but into the next as well. We all crept around like mice, not wishing to disturb him. I was so glad he had the lady Frida, for she was able to comfort him in a way no one else could, not just by her physical presence in his bed, but also by her calmness and gentleness. I noticed how often just a tiny touch of her hand on his would light up his face, briefly, before he was lost again in deep thought.

It was nearing the time when we would celebrate Martinmas that the news came that none of us could have anticipated and which finally sprang our lord into action.

A rider came galloping into the yard and dismounted.

"News for my lord Edmund!" he cried and I was sent hotfoot to find him.

I eventually tracked him down talking to the swineherd about bringing in the pigs from their foraging in the woods. He ran back to the homestead, with me struggling to keep up.

"I don't believe it!" he was saying, when I eventually panted into the hall. "This can't be true!"

"I have it on the best authority," the messenger replied.

My lord staggered to the nearest chair and flopped into it, gripping the arms to steady himself.

"And he's taken forty ships with him?" my lord queried. "Surely not?"

"It's true."

"Were they Thorkell's ships?" my lord asked.

"No. He still has his and, as far as we know, he's still in the King's pay and loyal to him."

"So these were ships raised through the levy on Mercia," my lord groaned. "How could he?"

He thumped his fist on the rim of the chair and scowled. I had never seen him so angry.

"God damn the man!" my lord shouted. "He was my father's most loyal counsellor. Curse him for his treachery!"

He reflected only for a moment, then leapt up.

"That's it!" he cried. "I must go south. Prepare to leave!"

We ran to fulfil our various tasks, knowing a long and miserable journey lay before us.

And it was truly miserable, for there was mist and mizzle and muddy roads and my lord moody and mad. We reached Winchester by the middle of the month and found the court buzzing with the news.

"It's not just the earl who's gone over to Cnut," Ealdwine told me, "but he's persuading other thegns to abandon the King as well."

"But I don't understand," I cried. "Earl Eadric was always there at the King's side. Why on earth should he join Cnut?"

"There's a demon in that man," the priest sighed. "The devil's at work in him."

174

"It's more straightforward than that," Aelfnoth chipped in. "I guess he reckoned the King was dying, the country would collapse and Cnut would walk in unopposed. Earl Eadric is the sort of man who wants to be on the winning side."

"He doesn't really care about the King then?" I asked.

"Care?" Aelfnoth scoffed. "He only cares about himself. He thinks Cnut's about to become king, so he's switched sides. He definitely doesn't care what happens to the King."

"And is the King alright?" I asked. "I know he's here somewhere."

"He's better," Ealdwine reassured me. "Fully recovered – at least for the present."

"And he's certainly well enough to be mighty angry," Aelfnoth added, "so young Wulfgar, I suggest you steer clear of him. He's lashing out at everyone."

I feared for my lord. He had come to offer his services to his father, but I wondered if the King would be grateful. Most of the court members were keeping their distance, gossiping in hidden corners, avoiding the King if they could, but my lord would have to speak to his father face to face.

I suddenly realised this would be the first time they had met since my lord had defied his authority and married the lady Frida. The King might even know about the diploma my lord had issued giving land to the New Minster here in Winchester. If he did, he'd be furious. So

I thought my lord was brave in coming here and facing the King.

"Who is that thegn my lord is talking to?" I asked Ealdwine.

He looked across the room at the stocky man with fair curly hair, a little older than my lord.

"That's earl Uhtred," he replied, "the Northumbrian lord married to Aelfgyfu, one of the King's daughters."

"Oh yes, I remember now," I acknowledged, "I saw him in Oxford."

"He's a bit of a hothead," the priest grumbled. "Not a good influence, I fear."

"Is he loyal though?" I pressed. "Surely that's what matters at the moment."

"He's not like earl Eadric. That man's sly and you can never be sure what he's thinking. Earl Uhtred ..." Ealdwine paused. "He's very likable because what you see is what you get."

"But not a good influence?" I queried.

"You know our lord's tendency to act and then to think." Ealdwine raised his eyebrows and smiled slightly. "Earl Uhtred is worse."

I couldn't see that really mattered. We were here to offer help to the King, and earl Uhtred's base was in the far north of the country, well away from Danish action this time round.

I was more bothered with how the King would react when he met his son. Of course, I wasn't there to see it, but I could tell when it had happened.

My lord had been fairly calm and also had seemed hopeful. After all, he had come to fight and how could the King be other than pleased about that? But it became clear the King was very angry. He was angry about earl Eadric and that was spilling over into everything else.

My lord obviously met with abuse, for his mood suddenly changed to one of anger and I was scolded for some trifling failure. I got no sympathy from Ealdwine either.

"You know it's a difficult situation," the priest chided. "Even if we do no wrong, my lord is likely to get cross. He's venting his frustration."

"The lady Frida would calm him down," I muttered.

Ealdwine nodded.

"Yes, she has a wonderful effect on him," he agreed, "but it would hardly have been appropriate to bring her to court."

"Perhaps we'll go home now," I suggested.

We did, and received news of a very different kind.

CHAPTER 20

We were nearing Christmas and I think we all felt in need of some kind of encouragement, a reason to feast, for our journey to Winchester had borne no fruit. My lord Edmund had been as moody on the way back as he had been on the way there, but the lady Frida worked her magic and he was soon smiling again.

It wasn't long before we discovered we were not simply celebrating the birth of Christ, but another birth was to happen. My lord had been told he was to be a father, so we had double cause to celebrate.

Through the dark nights of midwinter, news came to us slowly. It appeared Cnut and the earl were spending the Christmas season on the south coast and were not making any raids inland. But all that changed before January was out.

"The Danes are marching north," declared a messenger. "Dorset and Wiltshire are in no state to threaten them, so they're heading up into Mercia."

"To attack Eadric's own area?" my lord cried. "Surely not?"

"Earl Leofwine holds the area in southern Warwickshire," he was reminded.

"We must do something to stop them. I'll go south and call out the fyrd in Warwickshire."

Messengers were quickly sent to the leading men in the north of that county and we came later to Coventry to meet the force that had been raised, but it was soon obvious there was a reluctance to fight.

"Do you have the King's authority?" one thegn queried.

My lord was clearly taken aback.

"I don't need it," he responded. "We know the Danes are ravaging not that far away and we need to stop them in their tracks."

"The men won't fight," the thegn objected, "unless the King tells them to and there's help from London."

"Help from London?"

"Yes. They should come out of their stronghold and join us in the field."

My lord had no option but to send word to the capital and while we waited, the men of the fyrd kicked their heels and grumbled. It was a ridiculous situation. The Danes were harassing our fellow countrymen, but no one was willing to try and stop them. No wonder my lord paced up and down the hall where we lodged.

When word finally came, it was not good news. There was no support from the King or the people of London. Perhaps if there had been better relations between father and son, the answer might have been different.

"An aetheling has no authority!" my lord complained. "I try to stop our enemies from overrunning England and what help do I get? None."

He banged his fist on the table at which he was sitting and the cup of ale shivered at the blow.

"Right," he sighed. "Disband the fyrd. Send the men home." He paused. "We'll go east and try Northamptonshire."

I admired his tenacity, for he wasn't giving up easily.

Messengers now went east with dire threats to any who refused to respond to the call to arms. At the same time, my lord sent a letter to the King begging him to come.

Much to my surprise, the King did come, but with a strong bodyguard.

"What have you done?" he demanded.

My lord looked surprised by the question.

"Called out the local fyrd," he answered.

"Why?" was the next, rather angry, question.

"To fight the Danes, of course. They're just over the border harassing the lands of earl Leofwine."

"You have no right to raise the fyrd," the King shouted. "This is a plot to overthrow me."

My lord was speechless.

"You can't wait for me to die," his father continued. "You want to seize the throne and you see your chance by pretending to raise a force against the Danes, but really you plot to use it against me. You think that while I'm here, you can entice me into a battle where I will just happen to get killed and then you can claim the throne."

"No!" My lord had found his voice. "That's not true. I would never seek your death or encourage anyone else to do so. I am your loyal subject, as well as your son."

"I don't believe you," the King declared, "and that is why I am going back to London and you are ordered to disband the fyrd."

We were all stunned. My lord was trying to save the kingdom from the Danes and the King thought he was plotting his overthrow!

"Is the King ... mad?" I asked Ealdwine later. I knew people sometimes acted strangely when they got old and the King certainly looked very gaunt these days.

Ealdwine sighed and thought for a moment.

"Not ... mad, I don't think," he mused. "Since earl Eadric betrayed him, he's become paranoid, convinced *everyone* is about to betray him."

"But my lord wouldn't try to kill him!" I objected.

"No, but ..." He gave me a quizzical look. "Last autumn, he was ... rather acting like he was the king already."

The diplomas! I remembered.

"But that's not the same as killing him," I argued.

"No, I agree, and I don't think our lord would ever seek to ... hasten his father's death. But in these terrible times, men's loyalty is being tested."

My lord disbanded the force that had gathered and we prepared to go back north, but before we left, a messenger arrived.

"The devil he has!" was my lord's greeting to the news. "Right, that settles it. He's going to get some of his own medicine."

He sent the messenger ahead of us and by the time we reached the homestead in Derbyshire, men were beginning to gather. Was my lord again defying his father and about to take a force from the Five Boroughs against the Danes?

We soon discovered we were going north, not south. Near Chesterfield, we met armed men led by earl Uhtred. Even together, we were probably no match for the Danes, but it seemed we weren't heading in their direction. We turned west.

"Father, do you know what's going on?" I asked Ealdwine.

"I have a fair idea," he confessed, but said no more.

"Can you tell me?" I pleaded.

The priest sighed.

"The man who came to us at Northampton," he told me, "brought news of an attack on our homestead near Newbury."

"Oh, no!" I cried.

"No one was hurt," Ealdwine reassured me, "but earl Eadric ordered the burning of the barn and what remained of the winter fodder."

I was horrified. It was only late February and there would be several months before there would be more food for the animals and even the workers would be going hungry.

"I believe our lord and earl Uhtred talked in Winchester of making the earl suffer," Ealdwine continued, "and this mean act of his has prompted the two young men to act against him."

"But the earl is down south, not in the west," I argued.

"He has many homesteads around Chester, Stafford and Shrewsbury. I think that's where we're going."

"To do what?"

The priest shrugged his shoulders.

"Burn a few barns I guess." He shook his head. "It's a very rash plan in my view," he added quietly, "and I have told our lord so, but he is bound to earl Uhtred by an oath."

It was not a good time. No Englishman really likes to see his fellow countrymen suffer, but there was pent-up fury in some of the fighters and here at least was a way of dealing with some of their anger and frustration. I couldn't feel any enthusiasm for burning the earl's barns and was reminded of the campaign in Lindsey two years earlier. It was the Danes we should be hurting.

The destruction was cut short by appalling news. If earl Uhtred and my lord had hoped earl Eadric would speed north to defend his property, they were wrong. Their presence in the west had left Northamptonshire and the Five Boroughs vulnerable.

"Edmund!" earl Uhtred cried. "This messenger says Cnut's in York."

"York?!"

"Yes. He's brought an army up the east side of the country and seized York. He's threatening my lands. I must go back straightaway."

My lord nodded his agreement, but I could see the colour draining from his face.

"Cnut's in York," he muttered. "That means he's been through the Five Boroughs. Oh God, Frida, what have I done?"

Earl Uhtred hurried back to his base and we travelled fast towards Derbyshire, my lord terrified by what he might find and blaming himself for being so foolish. Ealdwine could have said, "I told you so", but I don't think he did. We were all afraid of what we might find. Almost every man had left behind a wife or a mother or a daughter and we knew the Danes' reputation for rape and slaughter.

Several days of hard travelling brought us within sight of the homestead. The buildings still stood, so there had been no destruction, but there was no smoke seeping out of the thatch on the hall roof, no signs of activity or people, no dog barked as we approached; there were just a few hens scratching in the dust.

"Oh God!" my lord cried. "The place is deserted!"

CHAPTER 21

We were very wary as we explored the homestead for signs of life. The hearth ashes in the hall were cold, suggesting no one had been here for a few days at least.

"Where is everyone? Where are the dogs?" my lord cried. "And where is my wife?"

"There has been no damage, my lord," Aelfnoth commented. "And no signs of ... of death. The animals are all alive."

"Surely Cnut cannot have taken everyone hostage?" There was a desperate tone in my lord's voice.

"We should get a fire going," Aelfnoth suggested. "And set a watch."

Several of our men were put to watch the trackways, while others gathered fuel. Early March was no time to be living without a fire. My lord also sent two men out to look for signs the Danes had been in the area.

Then, towards evening, one of the watchers brought in a lad he'd found skulking behind some bushes.

"It's the swineherd's son!" exclaimed my lord. "Tell us, lad, where is my lady and everyone else?"

"In thills," he replied, looking round suspiciously at the many faces he didn't know.

"Are they safe?" my lord demanded.

"Ah, we're all alreet. I saw smoke and came to see."

"And you can see, lad, that it is your lord returned, and with his men. Go quickly and tell them it is safe to return. There are no Danes here."

He smiled broadly at the boy, but the lad seemed reluctant to move.

"Wulfgar, go with him," my lord ordered.

So we went together. It was a fairly silent journey as I couldn't get him to tell me anything and I soon gave up trying. He led me through woods and almost hidden trackways into a hilly area riddled with caves. Here we found the makeshift camp created by the men of the homestead and here was the lady Frida, looking as beautiful as ever, especially once she heard news her lord was safely returned.

Before the light was lost, everyone was back in the homestead gathered around a blazing fire in the hall.

"We had news the Danes were coming," the lady Frida told us. "So we fled into the hills. My men know secret places there, so we were sure we'd be safe. Every day someone came back to check the buildings and the animals. We took the dogs with us to warn us of strangers."

"But the Danes never came?" my lord commented.

"We think they passed to the east," she replied, "but we had no way of knowing when they would go south again."

"They've reached York," he explained. "But you have a point. They'll surely not stay there and risk being cut off from their base at Poole."

That thought put something of a dampener on our reunion. The next day the men who had joined our campaign left us to return to their homes, but four had agreed to stay.

I was sharpening some quills under Ealdwine's eagle eye when we were joined by my lord Edmund.

"Ah, Wulfgar, I see you are ready to write a letter," he declared. "I need one doing."

He sat down by Ealdwine and I began to look for some parchment.

"Father, I've ... I've been very foolish," he confessed. "I did not think about the safety of my wife when I went off with Uhtred. He and I had made a pact and that was all I thought about."

"At least you came to no harm and neither did she," the priest commented.

"I know, but I fear to leave her here," my lord responded. "I want to take her to a safer place."

"Is anywhere safe these days?" Ealdwine queried.

"I have been thinking about that," my lord continued. "Well, I have prayed about it too and what came into my mind was Odda and his family at Deerhurst. The Severn is a deterrent to the Danes and they have no need to cross it. The family could easily escape if threatened and if I am not there to defend Frida."

Ealdwine was thoughtful.

"It does make sense," he acknowledged. "That is not an area the Danes have harassed. Their next target is more likely to be London, for if they capture the capital, they capture the land."

"Over my dead body!" exclaimed the aetheling. "But you're right. Their focus has to be on the major cities. They won't bother with a backwater like Deerhurst. So I'll get Wulfgar to do a letter in the hope that gets through, but we will set out anyway. I'm not waiting for the Danes to come back this way!"

In two days we were almost ready to leave, but then news came from York.

"The Danes have left the city," the messenger said.

"And which way are they travelling?" my lord asked.

"South, but beyond that I don't know."

"We must go," declared my lord. "I can't risk their coming back this way."

"There's something else, my lord."

"More news?"

"It's about earl Uhtred."

"Yes?"

"He was forced to submit to Cnut," the messenger related.

My lord sighed and commented, "He hadn't the force to fight him. I hope Cnut has treated him well?"

The messenger looked at the floor and shifted his feet.

"He's ... he's been murdered," he reported.

"No! By Cnut?"

"It's not very clear," the messenger admitted. "It may have been the act of a rival Englishman."

"Shame on him! Shame on whoever did this deceitful act! Uhtred was a good man. He did not deserve this."

There was now an urgency in our journey, but also a greater element of danger, for we feared meeting the Danish army as they returned to Poole. So we headed west, the four men joining our party as additional fighters. My lord sent out scouts ahead of us to try and secure a safe passage.

Somewhere north of Stafford we came upon a village which had several smouldering buildings. Our men trod carefully and we kept a tight group around the lady Frida.

"My lord, there's someone in this house!"

My lord Edmund gingerly approached, with an armed man at his side.

"It's an old woman," the searcher reported.

My lord went in and soon returned with news.

"The Danes were here, she says. She's bedridden and couldn't flee with the other villagers, but the Danes didn't torch her house. Perhaps they have some decency in them after all."

"They can't be far away then," Aelfnoth commented.

"They're taking a different route south it seems," my lord muttered, "and they're on our path. This isn't good."

"What if we cross the Severn?" Ealdwine suggested. "We should be safe the other side."

"We've got to get there first," my lord reminded him.

"There's a bridge at Bridgnorth," the priest remembered. "We used it last year."

"Yes, we'll go west and find the river," my lord declared, swinging himself back into his saddle.

His wife gasped.

"Dearest, are you alright?"

The lady Frida smiled and nodded.

"Your child is kicking as though it also were on a horse," she laughed.

My lord frowned.

"Don't worry," she chided. "It is nigh on two months yet before it will be born."

We quickly left the village and edged our way west. Certainly if we had continued south we would have run into the Danes, for our party was smaller than their army and thus travelling faster. God seemed to be guiding us and answering our prayers for a safe journey.

We reached the bridge over the Severn without meeting the enemy and we felt much safer once we had crossed it. Now we could hurry south without fear, though my lord still sent out scouts ahead of us. The villagers here had not been troubled by the Danes and thus were generous in their hospitality, so we made good progress.

We kept to the west of the Malvern hills, but our scouts did go up there. On a clear day they could have seen across the plain of Worcestershire, but although they could see the Severn pushing its way south through the fields and woods, they couldn't see what lay beyond and thus we had no idea where the Danes were.

As we came nearer to Tewkesbury, my lord sent a messenger ahead to greet lord Odda. He returned with news that we were expected and were welcome, so my letter had reached them.

The night when we all sat in lord Odda's hall and enjoyed his hospitality was a great relief. My lord smiled and laughed for the first time in weeks and the lady Frida also seemed pleased that her journey was over. None of us knew what might happen next, so this could be the place where her baby was born.

There was also a sense of relief when news came that Cnut and his army were back in Poole. But, of course, by his march to York and his unhindered return to the south coast, he had proved the English were no threat. The King had failed to raise an army to attack the Danes and had even prevented his son from blocking their rampage through the land.

Now Cnut had Eadric in his camp and possibly some other thegns too, then he could be confident that, come Easter and the better weather, he could trounce the English and be king, like Swein his father.

CHAPTER 22

"My lord," Ealdwine began, "I think you should go to London, to your father."

Word had come a week after Easter that the King was ill again.

"He doesn't want to see me," was my lord's surly response.

"Go anyway," the priest urged. "If he dies, you need to be in London and if he knows he is dying, he may choose to see you, but if you aren't there, he has no choice."

My lord grunted. I guessed he knew Ealdwine was right, but he didn't want to admit it.

"I know he has hurt you," Ealdwine continued. "He has always put you down and never seen your worth, but you have hurt him too."

My lord scowled.

"Go and be reconciled," was his chaplain's advice.

My lord walked out and Ealdwine sighed. He caught my eye.

"Prayer?" I asked.

"Yes," he agreed, "but the Lord never overrules a stubborn heart."

"He might soften it," I suggested.

He sighed again.

"You have no father, do you, Wulfgar?"

"He died when I was young; I hardly remember him."

"Perhaps it is better to have no father than a harsh one," the priest pondered.

"But hasn't my lord learned to be strong?" I argued. "Hasn't he learned what makes a good king and a good father?"

He looked at me sharply.

"You are wise beyond your years," he commented. "I think he will be a fine king and a good father, but he needs to go forward unhindered by baggage from the past."

The next day my lord was up early and told us we were leaving.

"We're going to London," he declared, and Ealdwine and I exchanged glances. "But if I'm not welcomed, we come straight back."

When we were ready to leave, the lady Frida came out to say goodbye and my lord took her in his arms.

"I hate to leave you when your time is so near," he told her, and we all looked at our feet as we waited for him.

"God preserve you, my lord," she answered. "My time is yet awhile and I have women here. It's important that you go to your father."

"Odda, you are to take good care of her," he commanded. "Within her may be a future king of England."

We all looked up and smiled and hoped he was right. He lingered in his farewell kiss, but eventually we were on the road, trusting the spies had not been wrong in saying Cnut was in the Poole area.

Our journey to London was uneventful and we were glad we had met no Danes, though we saw evidence of their pillaging. We settled into our quarters in the city.

"Ealdwine," my lord ordered, "go and find out how the land lies. Wulfgar, go down to Greenwich and see if Thorkell is there, but don't speak to anyone about it. Just snoop around."

I did as I was told and was reminded of my first encounter with the great Dane. More than two years had passed and I was confident none of the foreign mercenaries would recognise me, though I didn't think it would matter if they did. I didn't intend to be conspicuous.

The Danes were still there with some of their ships and they seemed to be particularly happy, for several were making jokes and laughing and some were singing. They almost looked drunk. I wandered into a nearby inn and got chatting to the innkeeper.

"They're a happy bunch today," I commented.

"Ah, not surprising," he responded. "Been paid." And he winked.

I wondered what he meant.

"Are they always like this when they get paid?" I asked casually.

"No. Been paid a lot." He smiled knowingly.

I still didn't understand, but was reluctant to appear too curious.

"They do well out of the King," I remarked.

He looked around and then whispered, "They'll do better out of a different king."

I felt a shiver go through me.

"But I'll be sad to see them go," he added. "I've done good trade."

As I strolled back, I pondered his words. It sounded as though he thought the Danes would soon be leaving, but I knew Thorkell was in the pay of our King. I was puzzled, but found myself unable to report my findings as my lord was nowhere to be seen.

"Aelfnoth, where's our lord?" I asked.

He shrugged his shoulders.

"Don't know," he responded.

Perhaps he's with his father, I thought.

The news in the city was that the King had taken to his bed soon after Easter Sunday, but no one knew how serious it was.

"He keeps getting sick," we were told, "but he keeps recovering. One day, he won't, but we don't know when that will be, so we're on tenterhooks."

The city didn't feel like that, for trade was as brisk as ever. Many had come to celebrate Easter and were enjoying the period of calm which had come after Cnut withdrew south. The peace felt unreal to me, for I couldn't believe Cnut wouldn't strike again and wreak havoc in our land as he'd done after Christmas.

I bumped into Ealdwine coming out of one of the churches.

"Father, is there any news?" I asked.

"The King agreed to see his son," he told me, "so I hope they are making their peace with each other."

"Or our lord will hurry back to his wife," I suggested.

Ealdwine grimaced.

"It is a very difficult situation," he acknowledged. "Our lord needs to be here, but his lady is nearing her time. I know where he'd rather be."

So did I!

"Maybe the King will recover," the priest continued, "and we will be able to return in time for the birth." He glanced at me. "I pray for her daily."

We both knew how dangerous childbirth was and this was the lady Frida's first child. She had had no children by earl Siferth, but had conceived a child by my lord very soon after their marriage. I was very pleased for them, but, like Ealdwine, I was concerned nothing went wrong. Her pretty face floated into my mind and I felt my heart beat a little faster. My lord was blessed indeed in the choice of his wife, but then I realised he might at that very moment be having to defend his marriage before his father.

I happened to be with Ealdwine when our lord returned to our quarters and so witnessed their conversation.

"It wasn't easy," my lord confessed, "but thanks for paving the way."

"I hope you were both gracious," Ealdwine responded.

"Gracious?" my lord grunted. "He scolded me for my marriage, but has not insisted that I put my wife aside. I told him she was with child and all he did was frown. I didn't apologise for marrying her."

Ealdwine sighed.

"It is the betrayal that has hurt so much," my lord added.

"He feels betrayed by you?" the priest queried.

"He feels betrayed by everyone!" My lord paused. "I assured him of my loyalty. But that business with Eadric has gone deep. It was a knife in the back from the man he trusted most. He's angry and who wouldn't be?"

"The earl has shown no change of heart that we know of?" Ealdwine asked.

My lord shook his head.

"As far as we know," he responded, "he's still with Cnut. I'd like to put a dagger through his black heart!"

"I hope you don't get the opportunity," his priest chided. "The Lord Almighty will take vengeance in due course. Do I presume we are staying in London for the present?"

"Yes," my lord confirmed. "My father is very frail. I really wonder if he can pull through this time. Wulfgar, how were things in Greenwich?"

When I told him what I'd found, he pursed his lips and frowned.

"I don't like the sound of that," he muttered. "I think I'd better meet with Thorkell."

"Behind the King's back?" warned Ealdwine.

My lord looked him in the face and raised his eyebrows.

"What option do I have? My father's in no state to negotiate with the Dane and if he has authorised him to be paid what was owing, I believe I need to keep these mercenaries on our side."

Ealdwine winced.

"Alright," my lord declared, "I know you're worried about how that will look. I'll involve Ulfketel and perhaps one of the Witan members, so that it doesn't look as though I'm stepping into my father's shoes while he's still alive."

"That would be wiser," Ealdwine agreed.

I didn't witness that meeting, but it must have happened at some point in the next two days, for I heard Thorkell had been seen in the palace complex and I doubt if he was visiting the sick King. I couldn't tell from my lord's expression whether any such meeting had gone well, but I was so curious to know that, in the end, I broached the subject with Ealdwine.

"Yes, they did meet and our lord was not alone," he told me, "but I get the impression Thorkell wasn't committing himself."

"So he's not promised to continue fighting for us?" I asked.

"No, he's made no promise, but neither has he said he's leaving." Ealdwine sighed. "It's a strange business, isn't it? Thorkell comes here, ravages our country, piles his ships full of booty and then changes sides." He was lost in thought for a moment. "What's to stop him changing sides again?"

It was a worrying possibility and may have been one of the reasons my lord was so distracted and quiet. Perhaps, too, he couldn't stop thinking about his lady.

We had been there about a week, when he came to Ealdwine.

"My father seems a little better," he informed him, "so I'm thinking of returning to Gloucestershire."

"Don't be too hasty," Ealdwine warned. "From what I hear, the King is very weak."

My lord groaned.

"I know, my lord," his priest added, "you are anxious about your lady, but even if you were with her, you could not help her. She is surrounded by good people."

"I'll give it another day," he growled.

Late the next day, while my lord was still thinking what to do, he was called to his father urgently.

"I hear, Wulfgar," Ealdwine told me, "that the King has kept no food down today and between his bouts of sickness is talking as though his first wife were still alive."

"Do you think he's going to die?" I asked.

"I don't think it will be long," he confided. "We shall be staying in London yet awhile."

At that moment, the Queen stormed into our room.

CHAPTER 23

When we saw the Queen, we dropped to our knees.

"You're his chaplain." She wagged her finger at Ealdwine. "He's stopping the King from seeing me!"

"My lady," the priest responded softly, "my lord Edmund would not do that."

"Well, the King won't see me," she complained. "He says I'm not his wife."

"My lady, he is very ill."

"It's a plot!" she screamed. "My son, my Edward, should be his heir, but your lord is poisoning the King against us."

"My lady, I know it is very distressing."

"Distressing?! My husband is dying and they won't let me see him!"

"I'll see what I can do," he promised, and she swept out.

He shook his head slightly.

"Second marriages often cause problems," he commented.

"But the aetheling Edward is younger than me," I responded. "Surely the Witan wouldn't make him king?"

"Who knows?" he muttered. "Well, I'd better go and see if I can get her an audience."

I think he must have succeeded, for he gave me a wry smile when I saw him later in the day and the Queen didn't bother us again.

The news of the King's desperate state had got out into the city and there was a hush everywhere. People still traded, but no one shouted in the streets and everyone talked in low tones.

The next day, being a Sunday, the churches were full of sombre folk, praying for their monarch. Ealdwine told me that our lord had stayed at his father's side, even sleeping on a pallet in the King's bedchamber. None of us could see the King recovering this time, so none of us were surprised that he slipped into a deep sleep.

Still my lord stayed at his side, while we waited anxiously for the inevitable news.

The Monday was St. George's day, but there were no celebrations, just the usual services to honour the saint. In the late afternoon, the bells were rung, slowly and sadly, so all London knew the King had gone.

"His life has been a long one," Ealdwine reflected, "and there was much good done in the early years, but these last twenty have been wretched and filled with trouble. We have been easy prey for the wolves."

"What happens now?" I asked.

"The Witan will meet tomorrow and decide who will be the new king."

I was at a loose end, mooching around with little to do, so at first light, I walked down to Greenwich – really as something to do, for I had no idea I was in for a shock. But I was!

I stood on the quayside and looked about me. Not a Dane in sight! No Danish ships at all – everyone had gone. I enquired at the inn.

"There's been more activity than usual of late," the innkeeper told me, "but I wasn't sure what they were up to. Now I know. They were preparing to leave. Slipped downriver on the night tide. Paymaster's dead, isn't he? Gone to find another."

"But the new king would employ them!" I cried.

"Not being given the chance," was the sardonic comment.

I returned to the palace with a heavy heart, wondering how I could find my lord and tell him, for the Witan was meeting. Around midday we were called into the main hall and found it thronged with people. Some looked like merchants and men of the city, while others I recognised as thegns and the old king's counsellors. My lord was sitting on a chair on the dais with earl Ulfketel to his right.

"The Witan has met," earl Ulfketel announced, "and we have chosen as king ... lord Edmund."

A cheer went up and then we knelt to acknowledge him. I thought he looked pale and tense, for I could see his hands were gripping the arms of the chair.

"Good people," cried the new king, "please stand. I have accepted this honour with a heavy heart. Partly I grieve for the loss of my father. Partly I know the huge task that lies ahead to free our land from the curse of the Dane who makes bold to shelter his boats in our waters.

Cnut is not a man who will take our gold and go home; he is a man who will take our gold by force and conquer us – if he can. Do you stand with me in our fight against him?"

"Yes!" we all cried, and we meant it.

Even as he spoke, he seemed to grow in confidence and when he challenged us, he looked every inch like a king. I was so proud of him, and proud to be his servant.

I knew, however, that I had news he wouldn't relish, but I had to get it to him. As the gathering began to break up I inched my way forward. I was nearly there when earl Ulfketel blocked my path.

"Not now, lad," he ordered. "The King is busy."

"But I must tell him something," I pleaded.

"It'll have to wait."

"It can't!"

I was getting desperate and I tried to get round him, but he was a big man.

"My lord!" I cried.

King Edmund turned and, seeing me, he scowled.

"Sire!" I shouted, even as the earl tried to drag me away. "Thorkell's gone!"

The scowl changed to a look of puzzlement. Then he stepped across.

"Leave him be, Ulfketel," he commanded. "Wulfgar, what is this?"

"I've been down to Greenwich." The words tumbled out. "Thorkell and all his boats have gone. They slipped away in the night."

He stared at me for a moment, then closed his eyes briefly before turning to the men around him.

"This is what I feared," he confessed. "Thorkell pledged his loyalty to my father, but won't give it to me."

"You think he's gone to join Cnut?" Ulfketel asked.

"That's my guess," the King replied. "Our spies will soon tell us." He grabbed a man by his arm and said, "Send to the Kent coast for news."

Then he was enclosed by the thegns and I was ignored.

The next day the old king was buried. There was a grand service at St. Paul's, but I didn't see much of it as there were crowds of people and I was too short to see over them. Hardly anyone could remember our country without King Aethelred for he'd been on the throne for nearly forty years. Some mourned his passing, but many felt there was a bright future with a new, young king who would be better counselled than the old.

The coronation of that new king took place two days later. This time I managed to get a better view. I had been given a new tunic and I was smart and clean. I even had my hair trimmed. The King's retainers had a place together in the church and, as one of the shorter ones, I was allowed to stand nearer to the front. Thus I witnessed the two Archbishops, Wulfstan and Lyfing, anointing my lord with the holy oil. At that moment, there was no sound in the building, no shuffling of feet, not even a cough – it was a sacred moment.

Later in the service, the thegns each pledged their loyalty, but before they did so, there were others who took precedence. My lord's only surviving brother, Eadwig, knelt in homage and received a warm smile from his sovereign. Then up the aisle came the Queen and her three children, Edward looking as sour as ever. She barely bent her knee and only mumbled words of submission. She was a grieving widow, but she was also an aggrieved mother, for the Witan had not chosen her son. This little group received no warm smile from my lord, simply a nod of his head, acknowledging their submission.

In the evening, we had a great feast and there was rich food and lively music.

"This could be the last feast for quite a while," Ealdwine commented to me.

"How so?" I asked.

"The new king has to deal with Cnut and that is no easy matter," he explained, "made all the worse by Thorkell's desertion."

"Is there any news yet?"

"None that I know of."

"Might our lord, I mean the King, go to Deerhurst?"

Ealdwine was silent.

"He would like to," he said at length, "but he cannot go until he has made provision to secure Wessex against the Danes."

"But that could take weeks, or even months," I argued.

"Indeed." He raised his eyebrows. "I fear the lady

Frida won't see her husband for a long time."

My face must have registered concern, for the priest added, "Don't worry, Wulfgar, she's not alone. By now she will have heard that her husband is king, for news such as this is carried fast. She will know he cannot go to her. She is not so weak as to demand his presence."

I couldn't help thinking about her, her pretty face set firm to see her through the crisis of childbirth without her beloved husband at her side. For a brief moment, I heard again her screams in the Oxford hall and wondered if, at that very moment, she was screaming with a different kind of pain.

CHAPTER 24

It was a week after Thorkell's departure that news reached us of his whereabouts. His boats had been seen going out of the Thames and then round Kent and into the Channel, which meant he had not gone home. There was also news that Cnut had set sail from Poole and was heading east.

"Wulfgar," the King addressed me.

"Sire," I answered, having briefly knelt.

"Wulfgar, my brother needs some weapon practice," he informed me. "You are about his height."

I was nonplussed. The aetheling Eadwig was tall, like his late brother, and lithe as a cat. I had seen him wielding a sword and he was a natural.

"I ... I'll try, sire," I stuttered, "but he's ... well ... he's very good."

The King frowned.

"No, he isn't," he responded.

"He's lethal with that sword my lord Athelstan left him," I argued.

Now he looked puzzled.

"Oh!" he suddenly laughed. "You thought I was talking of Eadwig. Yes, he's proving to be a good fighter. No. I meant Edward. He's about your height even though he's younger."

I had no option, for it was an order. So the aetheling Edward and I squared up to each other with our shields and blunted swords, for this was not a real fight. At least, it wasn't meant to be, but Edward was in deadly earnest. He had a soldier shouting instructions to him and warning him of my attacks. I had no such help! He had no qualms about hitting me, whereas I was loath to injure an aetheling and I think he knew that.

My advantage was that I was nimble on my feet and thus able to get out of his range quickly. He kept trying to push me up against the wall of the courtyard where we fought, but I would dodge round him to an open space. My sword caught him once on his leg, but it didn't draw blood for he was wearing leggings.

We fought for some time and I sensed he was beginning to tire, so I pushed my advantage and had very nearly cornered him when a shout from his tutor ended the fight.

"That's enough for today!"

Edward stalked off leaving me to check I was merely bruised and not cut.

"I heard you had to provide lord Edward with some practice," Ealdwine commented that evening.

I grimaced and said nothing.

"It's good, Wulfgar. He needs to learn to fight, for his life could depend on it. We may all have to fight soon."

"Even priests?" I queried.

"Yes, even priests – and abbots and bishops," he responded. "Unless we want to be ruled by Danes."

"Is there any more news?"

"Yes." He sighed. "It's not good either. The ships

208

met in the Channel."

"And?"

"And they did not fight. Clearly Thorkell and Cnut are now on the same side." He paused and frowned. "The combined fleet is heading east. We suspect they intend to attack London."

"I was there two years ago, when Olaf brought down the bridge," I recalled.

"The King won't let that happen again," Ealdwine reassured me. "He has strengthened it and it's guarded now in such a way that no boat could get near it. The Danes will not be able to come far inland with their ships."

The following evening, as we ate with King Edmund and his men, we were interrupted by news that a messenger had arrived.

"Send him in," the King ordered.

I was shocked to see a face I recognised. He had clearly ridden hard, desperate to reach London without delay. The King leapt up, for he too knew why this man was here.

"My wife!" he cried. "You've come from Deerhurst!"

"I have," panted the messenger. "All is well. Your wife has given birth to a son."

"Oh, praise God!" cried my lord and clapped his hands. "And are they ... are they both alright?"

The messenger beamed.

"Very healthy, sire."

"I have a son!"

The King looked around at everyone assembled and we were all smiles, for this was the best of news – the King had an heir, a new aetheling had entered the world. For the moment we rejoiced and gave little thought to the troubled nature of that world. Here was a fresh reason to fight for England and send the Danes back home.

The news the next day was not so good.

"So Southampton has chosen Cnut as King," my lord Edmund growled. "Only a few months ago, my father was defending the place from attack and now he's dead, they capitulate."

No one could think of anything to say, for it was a terrible rejection.

"Does this mean that most of Wessex is in Danish hands?" he railed.

I don't think he really expected any of us to answer him.

"Can I rely on the north?" he exclaimed.

"Sire," Ulfketel had found his voice, "East Anglia is loyal and your Five Boroughs will stand with you." He paused.

"And Mercia?" demanded the King.

"Earl Leofwine is loyal, though he commands less power than ... than Eadric."

"Do we know where that scoundrel is?" the King wanted to know.

"Not for sure," Ulfketel replied. "We think he's still with Cnut."

"If I get my hands on him, he's a dead man." He was quiet for a moment and then leapt to his feet. "Right, let's check the city's defences and our supplies. It won't be long before those dogs are yapping at our ankles. We need to teach them a lesson."

There was plenty to do, but I couldn't help feeling gloomy and I sought out Ealdwine before the day was out.

"We were here nearly three years ago," I reminded him, "when Swein swept through England. We weren't able to stop him. How is it going to be different this time?"

Ealdwine frowned and thought for a while.

"Swein had captured the north," he remarked, "and Cnut doesn't really have that. He's made a base in Dorset, not Gainsborough. But ... " He paused. "But he might try to besiege us. If he can capture London ... " He grimaced and shook his head. "We would be fleeing for our lives," he concluded.

"Could he capture it?" I asked.

"Cnut can't get his boats further up the Thames than Greenwich because of the bridge. The King has done a good job of fortifying that. But it will be difficult to bring him to battle and we could have a lengthy stalemate."

"I expect you're praying," I commented.

"I pray constantly. At least the lady Frida is safe and well and so is the child – and they are far from any fighting. I fear our King will not see his son for many weeks though. But I pray he does see him and that somehow peace could come to our land." He looked at me and there was great sadness in his eyes. "Greed is a terrible sin, Wulfgar. It grips a man by the throat and will not let him go. He desires what another has and cares not what price he pays to get it. God gives us what we need. Why do we have to try and grasp more?"

I blinked at him, for I certainly didn't know.

"Christ is the only answer," he continued. "If men could but make him lord of their hearts and lives, then we could live content and the whole world could be at peace."

Ealdwine was right about the bridge. Danish scouts did come upriver, but were soon beaten back and it was clear there could be no repeat of Olaf Haraldson's amazing feat. But there were enough Danes south of the Thames for us to stay inside London's walls. Was Ealdwine also going to be right about the lengthy stalemate?

I expect the King was consulting his counsellors, but I wasn't part of that elite and had to depend on picking up snippets of news. I couldn't imagine my lord would sit still for long, but what to do? In the end, his hand was forced.

CHAPTER 25

Word began to seep into the city that the Danes were up to something. Well, Cnut wasn't one to sit still either! What they were doing mystified us at first. There were reports of teams of men digging. A huge workforce, probably reluctant English labour, was being employed day and night creating a pit which was being extended at each end and thus turning into a channel. They worked fast – that's why I think they must have forced local people to do it or die. The whole of the area was teeming with Danes, though to us they looked like ants from our vantage points.

Then we realised what their plan was. They were making a channel to bypass the bridge and thus get their boats upriver. But it was no good sitting around admiring their engineering, for we could soon find ourselves trapped completely.

"The King wants us – urgently!" Ealdwine grabbed my arm and we hurried to his hall.

There we gathered with others of my lord's retainers, the men he knew best and whom he could trust. Included in these was lord Godwine, whom we had met in Sussex and who had been a loyal supporter of Athelstan and was now active on the King's side. But I noticed earl Ulfketel and lord Eadwig were also present.

"We can see what the enemy is up to," the King began. "Cnut's making a channel to get his boats past the bridge. We've looked seriously at what we can do, but believe we can't stop him. He could soon have London in a stranglehold." He looked around at us as we listened intently. "I need to raise an army to fight off the Danes," he explained. "London can withstand a siege for, say, a couple of months. I hope in that time to have enough men to relieve the city and push the Danes east."

Some men nodded in agreement.

"I'm leaving earl Ulfketel in charge here and my brother has also agreed to stay," he continued. "We need to give the Danes the impression that we don't have another plan. However, they'll probably learn soon enough that I'm busy in Wessex and not kicking my heels in London."

The door was flung open and in marched the Queen.

"I hear you're going," she accused, barely acknowledging that she was speaking to her new King.

"I plan to raise an army," was the cool response.

She looked around at us.

"Who is staying?" she demanded.

"Earl Ulfketel and Eadwig."

She stared at these two men for a moment before turning her attention to my lord.

"Take Edward with you," she pleaded. "He's like a caged animal and longs to fight. He could be safer with you than if he's left here."

The King frowned.

"If the Danes overrun London," she added, "the aethelings don't stand a chance."

The King continued to frown. I guessed he was reluctant to include a lad of eleven in his mission.

"Very well," he agreed, "but my task will also be dangerous. The Danes will try to stop me."

She nodded.

"I know," she conceded. "I'm grateful, sire."

She curtseyed briefly before sweeping out.

"He could be a liability," muttered lord Godwine.

"Wulfgar." The King summoned me forward. "I'm putting you in charge of lord Edward. You are to guard him with your life."

I knelt and bowed my head. I didn't want him to see my face, which probably showed that I thought I'd been given a thankless task. In charge of lord Edward! My heart sank.

The next day the Danes broke through the river banks and their new channel filled with water. They immediately set about getting their boats upriver, though it was no easy task. We were too busy to watch their progress, for we had horses and provisions to assemble. Then, as night drew on, we began to leave the city, in pairs and by different routes, so as not to alert any spies. In fact I believe a diversion was planned by lord Eadwig; he wanted to set a Danish ship on fire and cause a distraction, but whether he succeeded, I don't know, for I was too taken up with my new charge.

Lord Edward had looked down his nose when told I was his guardian.

"I don't need someone to look after me," he complained.

"You'll do as you're told," the King said. "Lives depend on orders being obeyed. If you can't do that, you'll stay."

Lord Edward muttered under his breath as he mounted his horse.

"Do you hear?" the King repeated.

"Yes, sire," the lad answered.

Lord Godwine took the two of us out to the meeting place north of the city. There we waited in anxious silence for everyone else. It was hard to keep the horses quiet. Aelfnoth was the last to join us.

"We were spotted by a Danish scout," he told the King, "but he won't be able to report to his lord – I cut his throat."

We hoped there hadn't been any other scouts we'd missed. Once we were all gathered, we moved off – slowly at first, but once we were well clear of London, we rode as fast as the moonlight would allow, the cool May night air keeping us awake and alert. Our group included the late king's bodyguard, his trained fighting force; these men were now King Edmund's.

We rode all night and reined in at a safe homestead just before dawn. Here we slept and rested, ready for another night's travel.

I took the King at his word and tried to stick closely to the aetheling, as I felt he should get used to my presence, even though he might resent it.

As we shared food later that day, he suddenly said, "I'll be king one day, you know."

"Really?"

"I can see you don't believe me," he scoffed.

Well, why should I?!

"The Witan chooses the king, my lord," I replied.

"And one day they will choose me," he boasted.

"How do you know?" I was genuinely curious.

"A monk told me."

"Like a prophecy, you mean?"

"Yes."

"Who was he?" I asked.

"I don't remember his name, but it was while I was at Ely."

I raised my eyebrows.

"I was educated there for a while," he explained, "and one of the monks told me I'd be king."

"I don't think it'll be just yet," I responded, thinking of my lord's youth and his newborn son – and there was the aetheling Eadwig.

"No, I'm not ready yet," he agreed, "but I must learn about being a king."

I reckoned he had a lot to learn – and that should include not being so pompous!

I didn't enjoy being his guardian, but I did find it had an advantage. The King usually included him among the people he consulted – not that lord Edward had anything to contribute, but I supposed it kept the aetheling out of mischief. Thus I too was often there when tactics were discussed.

"Once we're over the Thames," the King explained, "I'll send out my warrant to the reeves to raise the fyrd. That will be the first test as to how loyal the people are."

"I think you'll find, sire," lord Godwine responded, "that they will back you."

"But we had word Southampton had submitted," he countered, "and that involved both thegns and churchmen."

He glanced at Ealdwine.

"I agree with lord Godwine," his priest answered. "When the people see you – and see you at the head of a force, they will offer you submission."

"If all goes well," the King continued, "we head for Winchester. We must secure that city."

"Submission at Winchester will secure most of Hampshire," lord Godwine agreed. "Any renegade thegns could be isolated."

"Except there is access to the sea," Aelfnoth commented.

"Cnut may pursue us," the King pondered. "He could leave some troops besieging London and seek us out – if we are well received."

"If we are well received," lord Godwine argued, "we shall have an army to thrash him with."

"I need scouts, Godwine," the King told him. "I need

men to keep me informed of the enemy's movements. You have contacts in Sussex."

"Yes, sire. I'll put the matter in hand."

As we had hoped, we met no opposition. The area around Newbury welcomed us and men came with their weapons to fight for the King. We made good progress and had gathered a considerable force by the time we came near Winchester. Here, the King sent messengers to the leading citizens and soon the gates were opened and our force gladly provisioned.

As yet there was no news of Cnut. If he pursued us by boat, he had to come out of the Thames and round the Kent coast. May was slipping by fast and we all knew that our ultimate aim was to return to London and break the siege.

A major triumph was the submission of Southampton. Those in control there said they had been bullied into accepting Cnut and they now gladly submitted to King Edmund. Moreover, they promised to keep the town secure and would fight off any efforts by the Danish boats to use the harbour.

"News, sire," panted a young man, who tumbled into our hall at Winchester.

"Yes?" The King leapt up.

"Danish boats have been sighted off Hastings sailing west."

Lord Godwine was close behind him.

"We've also had news the Danes still have a

219

stranglehold on London," he added.

"Right, we move west too," the King ordered. "We need to secure Wiltshire and Dorset."

So we decamped, and the army headed for Salisbury. There we took more submissions of thegns and added more men to the force. We moved on to Shaftesbury and received the same warm welcome, but we also received news that Cnut's fleet had anchored at Poole.

"He'll move against us, I'm sure," the King said, "but for the moment, we'll continue our progress. We need to secure Bath, so we'll head north."

We had amassed a sizeable force by now and that meant we couldn't move very fast. A local man had advised we take the road to Bath via Gillingham, for he knew the route well and there was just a possibility of throwing Cnut off our scent – briefly.

The respite did prove to be brief, for we hadn't long passed through Gillingham when news came that the Danes were on our trail.

"We give battle," the King declared. "Now is the time to turn and stand our ground and bloody the Danish noses."

His words made me think of Aethelwine and his mutilated nose. Yes, that's why we were fighting. We didn't want these cruel Danes to rule our land. We had to force them to go home to Denmark.

CHAPTER 26

The place the King chose for our stand was at Penselwood, for the lie of the land was in our favour.

"Edward, you are to stay well clear of the battle, right away at the back," the King told him. "Wulfgar has my permission to stop you getting involved. You understand?"

"Yes," was the surly response.

"Yes, what?"

"Yes, sire."

"The only time you fight is if a Dane somehow gets close and you then fight to defend your life. Those are my orders and you will obey them."

King Edmund looked the lad full in the face. Eventually, my lord Edward lifted his eyes to meet those of his brother.

"I will obey your orders, sire," he replied quietly.

"The shieldwall is no place for youngsters," the King explained. "Men will die in this battle. We pray God it won't be too many of ours."

There was a strange light in his eyes. Certainly determination was there, but also fear – perhaps the right kind of fear, the kind that makes a man brave in the face of danger. As the shieldwall formed and we took our places well back where the carts stood full of supplies, I suddenly realised this was the first battle King Edmund had ever led. He'd fought in Lindsey, under the command of his father, but there had been no direct encounters with the Danes since his accession to the throne, a little over a month earlier. The ravaging we'd done in north Mercia had been altogether different. I prayed God would help him and would give us victory.

"Have you seen a battle before, my lord?" I asked lord Edward.

"No. Have you?"

"Only once – when King Aethelred went into Lindsey two years ago."

He didn't answer, perhaps he remembered too well being an exile in Normandy.

We were on slightly raised ground and so could see the troops getting into position.

"You'll see the King is in the centre flanked by his bodyguard," I explained. "They were your father's before. I expect you know they're a trained fighting force."

Lord Edward nodded though I wasn't sure he really knew.

"So the King has lined men up, shield to shield, to form a wall," I continued. "Cnut will do the same. Then they come at each other, trying to keep that shieldwall intact." I paused. "It's a noisy business, as well as deadly."

The King had chosen his ground well. All we needed now was for the Danes to appear – and choose to fight. And that's what happened.

Those in the vanguard were on horseback and as soon

as they saw us lined up, they shouted orders, dismounted and set about making their own shieldwall. It was midday before the two lines were ready to fight it out.

Again, it was the noise I remember, the yelling, the banging of the shields, the oaths and mocking. And then the screams. I glanced across at my charge. He was pale and trembling slightly. I couldn't tell whether he was scared or itching to get into the thick of the fighting. I knew I had no choice – my task was to guard him, not just from death but from capture, for he would be a very valuable hostage. The King could have done without this extra responsibility, but I knew that if the aetheling did have to fight, he would put in a gutsy and probably quite vicious performance.

Our shieldwall was holding, as far as I could tell, but there were men being pulled back out of it – usually the injured ones, for the dead were often left. We saw one man with a severed arm and my lord Edward was promptly sick round the back of a cart. I felt a bit sorry for him as he'd led a sheltered life, even if it had been uncertain and he'd gone into exile. He probably had never seen injuries like these. There were women and some men too old to fight who were at the back like us and they did what they could to help the injured. But it was clear we'd met a stronger force here than we had in Lindsey. If Cnut was here, he was obviously determined to fight hard.

We never discovered if the Danish leader had been here in person, for the fighting was fairly evenly matched and as the sun began to sink, the two forces fell back to rest for the night. We could count our losses – and they were high – but we still had a significant force determined to stand against the Danes in the morning. However, that never happened, for the enemy crept away in the night.

"Our scouts tell us the force is returning south, probably to Poole," lord Godwine reported.

"So, for the present, we have won," the King commented.

He looked tired – I guessed he hadn't slept much – but he also looked uninjured. His helmet, shield and mail coat had protected him and no doubt his sword had done its duty well.

"We'll press on to Bath, once we've buried the dead," he declared.

We had a sad day's work and there would be many families in Wessex who would go into mourning once they knew what had happened. But morale was good and people spoke well of their new King, for he fought with them and encouraged them greatly.

My lord Edward had little to say. I think the sight of so many dead and their horrific injuries and the smell of blood and urine had made a deep impression. I noticed he didn't eat much.

Two days later we were in Bath and received the submission of its citizens. Again warrants were sent out to local reeves to raise the fyrd and the troops we had got a chance for a brief rest. June is often a lean month for food, but the town was forced to supply provisions. I guess they hoped we wouldn't stay long and, indeed, the King seemed anxious to move on.

While we were in Bath, we celebrated the feast of King Edward.

"He was very young when he came to the throne," Edward the aetheling told me. "He was only my age."

"But he didn't reign for long, did he?" I asked.

"Four years. His stepmother had him murdered and that's when my father became king."

"He must have been even younger."

"He was – about seven – young enough to be controlled by powerful men."

I wondered if King Aethelred had ever ceased to be controlled by powerful men, and the earl of Mercia's face flitted across my mind.

"He's buried at Shaftesbury," lord Edward continued. "My brother took me to see his shrine while we were there. He has named his son Edward."

And he hasn't seen this child yet, I remembered.

"Miracles happen there," lord Edward was saying. "It's only a few years ago that my father ordered the observance of his feast."

As we heard the Mass, I glanced at the King. His eyes were shut and he seemed deep in prayer, but was he thinking of the tiny child waiting in Deerhurst with his beautiful mother? Was that why he was restless during those few days in Bath – inspecting and assessing the troops, enquiring about provisions?

"How far are we from Cirencester?" the King asked a local thegn the next day.

"About thirty miles, sire," was the reply.

"We hear the Danes are on the move again," lord Godwine warned.

"I'm not surprised," the King commented. "I presume they returned to Poole, licked their wounds and are now out to try again to crush us."

"The news is that a force is moving this way."

"We leave tomorrow," the King declared, "and with whatever men we have. Others can join us as we march."

"And are we going to meet them?" asked lord Godwine.

"No, we head north," was the answer. "Our scouts can keep us informed of the Danes' progress. We'll turn and face them at a place of our choosing."

The place of our choosing was near Sherston, about half way to Cirencester. Again the King chose a site that favoured our army.

Ealdwine said Mass and reminded us that it was the Feast of John the Baptist.

"It was the feast of St. Etheldreda yesterday," lord Edward told me afterwards, "but Father Ealdwine didn't mention her."

"Who's she, my lord?" I asked.

"She founded the abbey at Ely."

"I thought there were only men at Ely," I remarked. "That's where lord Eadwig hid in Swein's time."

"It is for men now," lord Edward answered. "It was refounded about three hundred years after St. Etheldreda died, but she has a shrine there. I've seen it," he boasted.

"Well, you'd better ask her to help us, while I'm praying that the King won't suffer the fate of John the Baptist and lose his head," I suggested. "This is going to be a tougher battle than the last one. The King says we can watch from a hill – if you want to watch."

"Of course I want to see what happens," he retorted, but I noticed his hand was shaking as he grabbed the hilt of his sword.

So, early the next day we took our place in a little copse on a hill where we could see but not be seen. It wasn't long before the enemy appeared, as we'd had word they were close by.

The two armies formed their shieldwalls and the shouting of insults began. We had a better view of the fighting than we'd had at Penselwood and could see how brutal it was. It was kill or be killed and it was hard not to wince every time we saw a man – on either side – severely wounded and fall. Often, once they fell, they were trampled on and stood no chance of survival.

After several hours, there had been no obvious winner, for both sides had hardly given an inch. A truce was called for the night and we all withdrew a safe distance to get some food and rest.

"Sire," said lord Godwine, "there are Englishmen fighting for Cnut."

"I thought as much," growled the King, "and the rat's among them, if I'm not mistaken."

"The rat?"

"Eadric, the traitor."

Others confirmed the Mercian was there, as were a couple of other thegns, whose names meant nothing to me.

"I think we have more men," the King commented, "but there were losses today."

Too many, it seemed, but a battle is cruel and some of the fallen were young men in their prime. Lord Edward was very quiet and the King barely noticed our presence. He was already thinking of tomorrow.

"If we can hold them for another day," he suggested, "they might feel sufficiently checked to leave us be. All these troops must mean the siege of London is weak."

"But we must get back there as soon as we can," lord Godwine advised.

The King made no comment. A lot depended on the morrow. There was a battle to be won first.

The next day, the scene was repeated. The weather continued to be dry and a bit warm for fighting.

"I think we have the edge on them, my lord," I commented.

Lord Edward looked where I pointed.

"Our line is definitely further forward than it was before midday," I added.

"Maybe," he muttered.

"You'll see how the King fights in the middle with his bodyguard," I continued, "and tries to make sure the flanks keep in line, so that the whole moves forward as one."

"Do you know what Cnut looks like?" he suddenly asked.

"No, I've never seen him, but he's nearly ten years younger than the King, so not even twenty."

We scanned the battle, but in vain.

"He'll have a helmet on," I concluded. "He may even be well back from the front line. If he got killed, the campaign would be over. The rest would go home."

Another hour passed.

"We are pushing them," I said gleefully.

Then, suddenly, there was a moment I'll never forget.

"Your King's dead!" a great voice shouted.

CHAPTER 27

Men stopped fighting in that instant and all eyes focussed on the speaker. He held aloft the head of a man and I thought of John the Baptist.

"Oh, God, no," I whispered.

"I'm Eadric of Mercia. I know your King and I've just cut off his head! Flee while you can!"

He held the head by its hair and for a moment I thought it truly was that of King Edmund, for it was a man of his colouring. Then I looked at the heart of our shieldwall and I was sure I could see the King's helmet. I was about to scream he was alive, when the King himself bellowed, "Eadric, I'm alive, but you're a dead man."

As he spoke, he hurled a spear at the earl, who barely dodged being hit, but it went right through another man and into a second one.

"Oh, he missed!" I breathed and turned to find lord Edward was not at my side.

Oh God, where is he? I thought, and started hunting in the copse for him.

He hadn't gone far. I found him behind a bush, retching.

Earl Eadric had thought to scatter the English by his cruel deed, but rather it gave greater vigour to our men and they fought well. A truce was called in the evening, though we had been close to crushing them.

"That man did look like the King," I confided in

Ealdwine. "I thought for a horrible moment he was dead."

"It was a despicable trick on the earl's part," the priest responded. "I knew that young man. His name was Osmaer. His resemblance to the King may have cost him his life."

"But many died again today," I replied.

"Yes, Wulfgar, too many. We priests have been busy dealing with the dead and dying."

"You said you might have to fight," I reminded him.

"I'm praying the enemy departs. Come, let's hear what our King has to say."

King Edmund gathered us around. His face was grimy with sweat and there was blood on his tunic, though I don't think it was his.

"We fought well today," he began. "I've told the men I'm proud of them. They kept the shieldwall intact and obeyed orders."

"You nearly killed the earl," lord Godwine commented.

"That rat!" he grunted. "At least no one fell for his ruse."

"I think the fighting stopped because of the horror of seeing a man's head displayed like that," lord Godwine responded. "Your spear throw spurred them on."

"We nearly had them. If they don't sneak away in the night, we must overwhelm them tomorrow, but for that I need every fighting man there is."

"I'll fight!" I cried.

231

"And me," lord Edward added, though with less enthusiasm.

The King looked at us and smiled.

"I value your support," he replied, "but you are both too young. You need to grow a bit more before you can join the shieldwall, otherwise your lack of height will create a weak point."

I think I was disappointed and I'm sure lord Edward was relieved.

Our council was interrupted by the entrance of a lady, who came and knelt at the King's feet. I noticed she was quietly weeping.

"This is John's widow," Godwine leaned forward to whisper.

"Ah," the King responded. He reached out and took her trembling hand. "Dear lady, I heard your husband fought bravely for me."

"He was terribly wounded," she managed to stutter through her tears.

"But sought to staunch the flow of blood and fight on, causing fear in many a Danish heart and a rattling of their bones."

"Sire, I seek a grant of land, for I have two fatherless children."

"And you shall have it," the King promised.

When she had thanked him, she gracefully withdrew.

"I pray I can keep that promise," he muttered.

We were all silent. I was thinking how messy and uncertain war was, but also how some men discovered they were brave.

"If the Danes go," lord Godwine broke the silence, "they'll head back to London. It's getting urgent we break that siege."

The King was quiet.

"We'll have to go east, sire," Ealdwine added, "not north."

There was a strange look in the King's eyes, which I couldn't read, but later Ealdwine whispered to me, "Wulfgar, do you know why the King was heading for Cirencester?"

"No," I confessed. "Is it a major town like Bath and Winchester?"

"No, it isn't that important." Ealdwine paused. "It is only about twenty miles from Deerhurst."

"Oh."

Realisation dawned on me. Of course, the King had not yet seen his son, who by now was nearly two months old. Nor had he held the lady Frida in his arms for many weeks. Whatever the outcome of the next day, it looked as though he would have to continue waiting.

As it happened, Ealdwine's prayers were answered; when we woke we found the Danes had gone.

"As we thought," groaned the King, "they knew they'd lose if they fought another day."

"Be thankful, sire," lord Godwine advised. "There'll

233

be no more loss of life. We can return to London – that's where Cnut will head."

I think probably only Ealdwine had guessed what the King had been hoping to do before returning to London, but really he had no choice, for every day was precious.

"London it is," he declared, and I felt his pain of putting country before wife and child.

So we began the march east. It was a slow business as men were tired from the fighting and some nursed wounds, but morale was high and the new young King was spoken of well.

We crossed the Thames at Wallingford on the fourth day and kept north of the great river on our way to London. We knew from our scouts that the Danes had put a great bank round the city. We also knew that Cnut's ships could probably get to London before we could. Even so, I suspected we had ways of letting the Londoners know we were coming, for word had come out that they were still resisting the enemy, so surely word could get in that the siege was nearly over.

I thought there could be a battle at London, but the Danes must have taken fright when they heard we were coming, for, again, they disappeared in the night and deprived us of the opportunity of thrashing them. We were able to march into the city unopposed and receive the cheers of the people.

I say "we" meaning the King and his retainers. Most of the army we'd gathered in Wessex was left north of the city to guard that area and thus allow the citizens to move in and out and replenish supplies. The siege had lasted just over two months.

"Now that the city is free as far as the north is concerned," the King explained, "we need to free up the river, so that trade can flow again."

"These troops are tired," lord Godwine commented. "They are looking for a reward and then to return home."

"I need them to throw the Danes out of their camp at Brentford," the King replied, "then they can take their spoils and go home." He paused. "But I'll need to raise fresh troops to clear the Danes from Kent."

"Perhaps it's Mercia's turn to help. How about raising the fyrd in the Oxford area as well as in northern Wessex?"

"That's a good idea, Godwine. But first let's take a day's rest before we attack Brentford."

So, two days after raising the siege, we moved the army west. We could see the Danish camp the other side of the Thames. I think we had taken them by surprise for they had numerous tents and supplies there from what we could see, and had made no effort to move these. Also it was very early and our troops had travelled under cover of darkness.

A shout went up when they saw us and they began searching for their shields and swords, but a vanguard rode over the ford on horses and a sizeable shieldwall was in place before the enemy was ready.

Edward and I were on horses and passed through the water easily, while others waded through. It looked to me as though there wouldn't even be a fight as we clearly had the upper hand and they were panicking.

Then I caught sight of two men on horseback, way over to my right.

"Lord Edward," I cried, "that's Thorkell the Tall. I recognise him."

I pointed out the men.

"Is that Cnut with him?" he asked.

We stared at the two Danes, who were watching our shieldwall, rather than looking at us.

"It could be," I said. "He looks young from here."

Suddenly, lord Edward dug his heels into the flanks of his horse and galloped at them. He unsheathed his sword and raised it menacingly.

Oh God! I thought. What's he doing?

And I galloped after him.

CHAPTER 28

The two Danes appeared to be frozen – perhaps it was the shock of seeing a lad on a horse coming at them full tilt or perhaps they were too deep in discussion about what to do. I'll never know why they didn't move or why they didn't unsheathe their swords too – for they didn't.

Lord Edward was nearly at Cnut when Thorkell, at least, woke up and pulled his lord from his horse onto his own – just in time, for lord Edward's sword slashed into the saddle straps and into the flesh of the horse.

The horse gave a sickening neigh and bolted, but Thorkell had Cnut on his own beast and was racing away too. Lord Edward was temporarily winded from delivering such a strong blow and I was able to grab the reins of his horse and pull us back to our own troops.

By the time I had got us back behind the safety of the shieldwall, the fighting was over, for the Danes had fled, though few had horses like Thorkell.

This was what the fyrd had wanted. These farm workers, farriers, blacksmiths and the like were not trained to work as an army. They could put up a fight when called to, but true discipline was not there. And now that lack showed. They wanted to go home with booty and here was a Danish camp full of good things being hastily abandoned.

There were a large number of men who were still the other side of the Thames and they wanted their share.

People were plunging into the water regardless of whether it was fordable at that point. It was chaos!

I didn't see it all because I was trying to control our horses and keep lord Edward from getting into more trouble, for I feared he would try to chase after Cnut.

"What did you do that for?" I shouted.

"If I'd killed Cnut, that would have been it," he panted. "The Danes would have gone home."

It was a mad, wild gesture, but I had to admit he'd showed much more courage than I thought he possessed.

Behind us the river was becoming a death trap. Men were disappearing beneath the cold water and not coming up again. Others were panicking and pushing their fellows under in an effort to keep themselves from drowning.

Meanwhile the King and his bodyguard were maintaining the shieldwall, as they could be in danger if they pushed too far ahead of the rest of the army.

The Danes, however, were unaware that some of our men were drowning. They were following Cnut and Thorkell and fleeing for their lives.

When the King realised what was happening in the river, he broke up the shieldwall and called on folk to help the drowning, but even so, many lives were lost that day – all because they were greedy for plunder. It was a sad victory.

I wondered if I should tell King Edmund about his brother's attack on Cnut, but I didn't have to, as others had witnessed it and word had reached him by the time we regathered ready for the return to the city.

"What were you doing, breaking rank to go after those Danes?" he demanded.

"Wulfgar said it was Thorkell the Tall and I thought the other could be Cnut," his brother responded.

"It probably was," the King conceded, "but that doesn't mean you can go galloping at him."

"But if I'd killed him, it would all be over now for the Danes," lord Edward argued.

"It's a miracle he didn't kill you," was the angry response.

I thought I might get the blame, but the King didn't say anything to me. Lord Edward didn't speak to me either; he was sullen and silent all the way back to London. There, he was handed back over to his mother to whom he no doubt recounted his tales of being with the King, with suitable embellishments and subtle omissions.

We spent some time in London making sure there was a full recovery from the two months of siege and also trying to free up the city's trading routes, but, as the King had anticipated, the Danes were unwilling to retreat far. They took their boats downriver, but we knew they were lurking near the Isle of Sheppey and that meant they had a stranglehold on the Thames and the river couldn't be used by our boats – well, not unless they wanted to be attacked by the Danes!

"I need to go and raise more troops," the King eventually declared. "If the Danes return in my absence, I believe London can hold them at bay."

So we prepared to leave, and this time we didn't have to do so in secret. There would be spies in London, who would after a while get the news of our movements to Cnut, but we also had spies who could tell us if the Dane moved his troops upriver again.

"Wulfgar, lord Edward is staying in London," the King told me, smiling slightly. "He'll be safer with his mother."

I think he winked as he said that.

We travelled north at first, calling out the fyrd in the Watford area. The local thegns were ordered to find fighting men and take them to London. There was some reluctance as it was now late July and harvest time, but the King's orders had to be obeyed.

We then moved more towards the west, to the Aylesbury area with the same commands. And so to Oxford. Of course, we were in Mercia here, but Eadric wasn't here and had lost his grip on power, which meant the local thegns submitted and agreed to raise men and take them to London.

By mid August we were at Swindon.

"We came through here, didn't we?" I asked Ealdwine. "After the battle at Sherston."

"Yes," he confirmed, "so some of these men have fought already."

"Where might we go next?" I enquired.

"Cirencester?" he suggested, with a smile.

"Oh, yes, we're near Deerhurst again!"

We were both wondering if the King might, this time, manage to see his wife and child, but it was not to be. He may have hoped to achieve a meeting, but word came that London was under attack again. Therefore we had to gather what troops we could, march back across the country and meet up with others who had been called to fight.

"We've done this before," I commented to the priest. "Is this what life will be like – pushing the Danes away, gathering the fyrd and discovering they've come back while our backs are turned?"

He grimaced.

"It looks like that, Wulfgar," he agreed. "The Danes are showing no signs of giving up the fight."

"Could we pay them off?"

"The late King managed to do that sometimes, but Cnut seems far more determined to grab England for himself and stay." He paused. "It may come down to one decisive battle."

These words hung in the air for quite a while and kept coming back into my mind. This time Mercia and Wessex would give us a large fighting force and perhaps with this we could finally crush the Danes.

All our troops had been told to gather near Brentford and it was a great encouragement to see the force assemble.

It was nearly two months since the last time the King

had led the army across the Thames at Brentford and it was done very differently on this occasion. There was no rush to get over the river; the crossing was orderly and sensible. But, then, there was no longer a Danish camp to plunder. The enemy had heard we were coming and had retreated, even though they had attacked London from the south while we'd been away. The city had resisted and had been in no serious danger of falling, but the actions of the Danes showed how determined they were not to go home.

I felt for the King. He'd been crowned just over four months and he'd had no days when he could relax, for the Danish threat was unrelenting. Could peace *ever* come? I wondered.

We moved through the area south of London. This had once been occupied by the enemy, but now all we found were English relieved to be free. We headed for Kent and had reports there were Danes not far away. They turned to face us at a place called Otford.

I expected something like Sherston with many dead on both sides and two exhausted armies finally deciding they'd had enough, but it wasn't like that.

It started with the usual shieldwall and the insults and the shouting and then the horrendous clash of shields and weapons and the screams of pain. But the English had more confidence and more determination. Perhaps Cnut and Thorkell weren't there to give a valiant lead. I have no idea. What I do know is that we broke them fairly quickly and they began to flee.

It took great skill on the part of the King to keep control of the army, but he did it and even managed to pursue the enemy.

Anyone who couldn't get away from us was cut down there and then. We left a trail of dead behind us. Hardly any English had died or been badly wounded. The number of dead distressed Ealdwine, but exhilarated me, for I felt this could be it – we had the Danes on the run. They were about to be pushed onto the Isle of Sheppey and there they would either die or escape in their boats.

We were taking a rest at Aylesford when a totally unexpected message came to the King.

CHAPTER 29

Late in the evening, I was stopped in the street by a priest.

"You're one of the King's men," he said. "Please take me to his chaplain."

I looked at the man who seemed vaguely familiar, but I couldn't place him. He was thin and gaunt and his wizened hand gripped my arm.

"Which one?" I asked. "He has several."

"The one who's been with him for many years. The old, grey-haired one. He was with him at Tamworth."

Tamworth? Still I was puzzled.

"Ealdwine probably," I replied and we set off together.

As we walked in silence, I was dragging through my memory for Tamworth and this priest I was sure I had met. I quickly found Ealdwine.

"I need to speak to the King," the stranger announced.

Ealdwine raised his thick eyebrows.

"You remember me, don't you?" the thin priest continued. "We met at Tamworth. I serve the earl of Mercia."

Suddenly it all came back to me – this was earl Eadric's chaplain and he'd been there when my lord Edmund tried to get the Mercian to fight with him.

"But the former earl of Mercia now serves Cnut," was Ealdwine's frosty reply.

"I have a message. It's very important. Please."

Ealdwine hesitated for a moment, then turned to me.

"Do you know, Wulfgar, where the King is?" he asked.

"I think so," I answered.

"Then take us to him," the chaplain requested.

Having brought the two priests to the King, I decided I was going to hang around, unless I was told to leave, for I was consumed with curiosity. What was this man doing here? I couldn't imagine.

Ealdwine had positioned himself so that if his fellow priest had come intending to harm the King, he could step between them. The visitor, however, did not seem anxious to come too close.

"Sire," the priest began, "I am Alkmund and I come from Eadric, who served your father as earl of Mercia."

The King looked him up and down and also straight in the eye.

"Yes," he said warily, "I remember you, Alkmund. I am surprised to see you here."

The priest shifted from one foot to the other and kept clasping his hands together and then releasing them.

"I am surprised too," he confessed, "but I have served the earl for many years and assure you this is serious. It is no whim."

"Speak then," the King encouraged.

"The earl has been examining his conscience," he explained. "I have heard his confession, but he requires me to reveal to you that he is troubled."

King Edmund made no comment, but continued to stare at the messenger.

"He is heartbroken that he abandoned your father and ... and has been fighting with your enemies."

"Heartbroken?! He's a cursèd traitor!" the King cried.

Alkmund nodded and lowered his head, as though in shame.

"He seeks forgiveness for his ... his failure."

"He does what?!"

"He regrets joining the Danes," Alkmund asserted.

"I expect he does – now they're losing!" was the King's response.

"He craves your forgiveness and asks to be allowed back into your fellowship – and back into your army."

"You can tell that rat ...," the King began, but Ealdwine had touched his arm.

"This offer needs to be considered, sire," Ealdwine whispered, but I heard him and I'm sure Alkmund did too.

The King frowned.

"Wulfgar," he ordered, "take Father Alkmund and find him a bed for the night." He turned back to the priest. "I will give you an answer in the morning."

I did as I was told and therefore missed what I expected was a lively discussion between the King and his chaplain. I had to wait until the next day when I knew the visitor had left Aylesford before I caught up with Ealdwine.

"Father, what happened? Can you tell me?"

Ealdwine looked around, apparently not wishing our conversation to be overheard.

"Father Alkmund has been told that the earl may return," he said quietly. "The King will meet him after the Danes have been flushed out of Sheppey."

"But he's a traitor!" I exclaimed. "Think of his actions at Sherston. Even you said that was despicable."

"It was," he agreed. "He has acted dishonourably ever since he left King Aethelred and went over to Cnut. He has been a traitor." He sighed. "But what should King Edmund do?"

"Tell him to jump in the Thames!" I suggested. "With all his armour on."

Ealdwine smiled.

"That is the sort of thing the King wishes to say," he acknowledged. "Probably with a few oaths and expletives added."

He looked out across the yard where men were preparing to march on, mopping up straggling Danes and forcing the rest to take to their ships.

"The Christian faith is about forgiveness," the priest said at last. "We are all failures. We all make mistakes. That is why Christ came and why he died on the cross for us. We too are called upon to forgive. Every day we pray as our Lord taught us, 'Forgive us our trespasses as we forgive those who trespass against us'. How can God bless our King if he has unforgiveness in his heart?"

"But the earl is such a devious man," I complained.

"He smiles even as he is preparing to stab you in the back."

Ealdwine was thoughtful.

"How can the King trust him not to turn traitor again?" I argued.

"I know," he sighed. "We cannot know how genuine his remorse is. But what is the alternative?"

He spread out his hands in a gesture of despair.

"If the King had rejected his offer, the earl would have no option but to stick with the Danes and remain his enemy," he explained. "As it is, if he now comes over to our side, we have the advantage of the forces he commands."

"We can beat the Danes without him and his men," I asserted.

"Perhaps. But better to have him fight for us than against us."

I could see the logic of the argument and I could also see that Ealdwine would encourage King Edmund to act within the will of God, but I felt uneasy. I didn't like earl Eadric and I determined to try and keep out of his way.

The earl would have to wait, for we were busy completing the campaign. We pressed on, killing any Danes we found and confiscating their horses and equipment, but most of them had had the sense to flee, so we had soon flushed Sheppey clean of Danes. I was elated! We had done it! There were no Danes, well none that were alive, left on English soil. Of course, they might try to land elsewhere, but I wasn't thinking about that.

We returned triumphant to Aylesford where the King must have met up with the repentant earl, for when we all reached London a few days later, the earl was in our company.

The King made it very clear to the court that he had forgiven earl Eadric and therefore no one was to take revenge. He was now to fight for us and not against us. I noticed, however, that the earl was never alone. He had three of his retainers with him wherever he went. They were like a bodyguard, protecting him from anyone who had reason to kill him. I wouldn't have done it, but I'd have been pleased if someone else had put a knife in him.

The army the King had raised in Wessex was now disbanded and sent home. We spent several days making repairs to our equipment and finding fresh horses.

"Father Ealdwine," I asked, "I've heard the King has called up an army now from London. Have the Danes landed somewhere?"

"We haven't heard so yet," he replied, "but the King expects them to." He looked at me sadly. "They haven't gone home if that's what you thought."

"I hoped they had," I admitted. "I thought earl Eadric's defection and our trouncing of them in Kent might make them give up."

"I fear Cnut will never give up as long as he lives," the priest sighed.

"So we've got to kill him!"

"I expect we'll go with the King when we get word, but I doubt you'll ever get near enough to the Danish leader to cut him down."

"Lord Edward did!" I countered.

"The foolish boy," he muttered. "Cnut won't let *that* happen again."

"I expect you've heard what they are calling the King now?"

Ealdwine smiled. "You mean Ironside?" he asked.

"Yes," I agreed. "I think it's a wonderful nickname."

On 13th October, the King announced we would be marching north the next day. I knew we were ready, but was still surprised and said so to Ealdwine.

"I think the King had been planning this for several days," his chaplain confided, "but he has chosen to say very little lest our enemies get wind of his plans."

"Do we know where the Danes are and where we're going?" I asked.

"I don't know, but the King almost certainly does. What I have learned," he continued, "is that he's leaving lord Eadwig here and also lord Godwine, just in case."

"In case what?"

It was a silly question for I knew the answer.

"In case none of us return," was the priest's quiet response.

"But earl Eadric travels with us?"

"Yes." Ealdwine frowned slightly. "Perhaps the King feels safer having him within his sight."

I said nothing. I would have chained him to a wall in London. But, on the other hand, he commanded a significant force and perhaps we needed them.

So we left London and took an old Roman route north-east into Essex. We travelled for three days and then rested.

"Where are we?" I asked Ealdwine, as we gathered round the King that evening in a barn.

"This place is called Assandun, the Hill of the Ash Trees," he told me.

"The Danes aren't far away," the King informed us. "They left their ships to the east and went west into Mercia. Now they are returning, no doubt weighed down with their plunder."

He looked around at us – his bodyguard, earls Eadric and Ulfketel, some thegns I didn't recognise and several churchmen. With the men outside, now resting in makeshift shelters, we were a substantial army, larger than any the King had raised before. This was to be a decisive battle I felt. This time we'd kill Cnut and that would be the end of the Danes; I was sure that was the King's plan.

"I have news they are about a day away," he continued. "To our west is the River Cam. I reckon they'll cross it at Chesterford, and then come up the valley to this ridge. From here they will be looking for water flowing east, for we occupy a watershed. Our task is to make sure they never find that water."

There were nods of approval and murmurs of assent.

"Bishop Eadnoth is here to bless us, as is Abbot Wulfsige from Ramsey," the King explained. "Monks from Ely have come south with holy relics to aid our fight. But God would also have us create a strategy."

He paused to make eye contact with most of us there.

"Eadric, you will take the right flank with your Magonsaetan fighters, while, Ulfketel, you will take the left flank with your men from East Anglia. I will hold the centre with my bodyguard. The rest of you will reinforce the shieldwall and fill any gaps." He paused. "We have to crush them this time, but because we are between them and their ships they are likely to fight like cornered cats."

The whole camp was ordered to restrict movement the next day, for if we caused the birds to rise up suddenly in fear, we could warn the Danes of our presence. So we rested and waited.

That evening the Bishop celebrated Mass for us all and prayed for victory, though men also prepared to die and thus made their peace with God. There was no raucous laughter or the telling of jokes and riddles. The atmosphere was subdued for we knew that for some this would be their last night of sleep before they slept eternally. No one spoke about it, but I guessed every man thought it and remembered his loved ones left behind in London and elsewhere.

"We know the Danes have crossed the Cam," the King told us. "They will find us waiting for them at the top of the ridge. We think they probably know by now that we are here. We have been able to silence a few of their scouts, but our army is too large to hide. We can expect a fierce battle to begin before noon. We outnumber them, but that doesn't mean victory is assured."

Later, he took me on one side.

"Wulfgar, I want you to look after the horses. There's a slight rise in the land to the north. Remain there with the horses away from the battle, but if the fighting shifts, you'll need to shift too. I've told Ealdwine to be there too, for he cannot minister to the dying while we're still fighting."

I nodded. I thought him calm and very determined. Whatever happened, he had risen to the challenge of being King and of leading his people in war. He had truly earned the name Ironside. I felt proud to be his man, though frustrated I was still too small to fight.

"You'd better wear some protection," he added, "and have your seax to hand. None of us knows what will happen tomorrow, even though we have asked God for victory."

The 18th of October was dry and cool, good conditions for fighting. The shieldwall was formed and as the King expected, the Danes came into sight aware of our presence and ready to do battle.

I don't think I'll ever get used to the sound of war – the clash of shields and weapons, the screams and shouts.

There were ash trees on the small hill where we waited. Some were still in leaf so we were screened from our enemies, but we could see enough. I think Ealdwine was quietly praying for he didn't talk to me and I had to deal with my fears alone.

It was true we outnumbered the Danes, but still we made little impression – both sides seemed evenly matched when it came to the actual fighting. The shieldwall moved backwards and forwards and my emotions went down and up in the same way. I could see men being cut down on both sides, the King and his bodyguard were solid and strong.

All of a sudden, after perhaps a couple of hours, there was a movement on the right. The Mercian flank appeared to be breaking up.

"Father, look!" I cried. "Something's wrong!"

CHAPTER 30

Ealdwine looked where I was pointing. Men were scattering, pulling back from the shieldwall and running north.

"It's earl Eadric and the Magonsaete," the priest gasped. "They're fleeing. Oh God, no! This is a disaster!"

The shieldwall shuddered to a halt and both sides parted briefly, aware that part of the wall on the English side had collapsed. An unexpected hush fell over the battle, as though everyone wondered what would happen now. I could feel my heart pounding in my chest and my mouth was dry. Then a voice came clear and strong.

"Englishmen," cried the King, "today you fight or surrender yourselves altogether. Therefore fight, I say, fight! Fight for your liberty and your country!"

I saw him lead his men forward into the heart of the enemy and I could see the sunlight glinting on his great sword. His bodyguard went with him and the left flank of East Anglians also shouted their support and followed his example.

Without the Magonsaete perhaps we were more evenly matched in numbers, but their departure was a terrible blow and we could make little headway against the Danes.

"Why's he gone?" I asked. "We weren't losing."

The priest shook his head slowly.

"Fear or ... betrayal," he responded.

"He planned it? You think that?" I was aghast.

"I don't know," Ealdwine acknowledged, "but he has put our cause in grave jeopardy."

We said no more. The King's words had spurred on our men, but the Danes were fighting very fiercely. Their army was smaller, but each one of them was a fighter, whereas ours was a combination of trained fighters, thegns and men who rarely wielded weapons in war.

I went into a small wood back from the battle line to relieve myself and as I returned towards our lookout position, I realised I could hear the sounds of weapons clashing – not just in the distance but close by. There was a Dane attacking Ealdwine.

The priest was putting up a good fight, but he wasn't made for war. I was going to have to do something.

The Dane had his back to me and I could see he wasn't so well protected there. I quietly drew my seax and crept up behind him, making sure he couldn't see me though I think Ealdwine realised I was there.

I was going to have to kill him, otherwise he'd kill Ealdwine and then me, for I'd stand no chance against his brawn and skill. My heart was pounding and my mouth dry. I braced myself.

Then I lunged at him and struck my seax up his arse. His scream was terrible. As he lurched in pain, Ealdwine put his weapon into the Dane's stomach and blood spurted from our enemy's mouth.

I withdrew my seax and tried to wipe the blade on the undergrowth, but my hands were shaking violently.

"Thanks," panted Ealdwine, "you saved my life."

I couldn't speak. Never before had I killed a man and I didn't dare look at his face in case he was young.

"An old campaigner chancing his arm for booty," the priest commented and I felt a bit better.

We pulled him to one side and took up our lookout again.

"Wulfgar, the battle is shifting towards us," Ealdwine soon warned. "I think we should lead the horses further to the north or we may find ourselves overwhelmed."

He was right. The Danes were advancing slowly and our task was to keep the horses safe in case of rapid flight. Thus we lost the advantage of the high ground and sought cover in the small wood and so lost too our view of the battle. We could still hear it though and could tell we were not defeating them.

As the light began to fail, so the sounds lessened and after a while we were sure a truce had been called for the night. Tentatively, we ventured out from our shelter to find the remnant of our army a little way to the east and the Danes withdrawing a short way south.

Ealdwine was anxious to find the dying, but they were everywhere. I had never seen, in any of the battles, so many bodies strewn across the earth, men with only half a face, or part of an arm, blood oozing from huge wounds, the moans of pain and despair.

I wondered how anyone had survived and began to fear the King had died, but I found him alive with several of his bodyguard in a huddled conference.

"That rat has done for us, I fear," he was bemoaning. "Ah, Wulfgar, the horses are safe?"

"Yes, sire, we took them into the wood," I answered.

"Good. We may need them, for I have lost some good men."

He was sitting with hunched shoulders, his sword still unsheathed and I could see it was covered with blood, as was his clothing. I thought it a miracle he appeared to have no serious wounds.

"Ulfketel – he was a good man and a good fighter. May God rest his soul," he added, sighing deeply. "And Aelfric and Athelweard. God, the flower of England has died today!"

A monk crept into our group.

"What news?" asked the King.

"Both the Bishop and the Abbot are dead," he reported, and I could see he had been weeping.

The King shook his head. It was a gesture of despair I thought.

"We are beaten," he concluded. "We might have done it if that rat hadn't fled."

"The Danes were like wild animals," one of his bodyguard commented. "They raged as they fought. They meant to kill or be killed."

"We must flee ourselves," the King said. "If we stay,

we'll be dead men before the sun reaches its zenith."

He looked at the monk, who seemed to read his face.

"We will stay, sire," the monk responded. "If the Danes do not kill us, we will take the Bishop and the Abbot back to Ely after we have buried the other dead here."

"I'm grateful to you for your loyalty and your courage," was the King's quiet but firm answer. He turned to a retainer. "Take the word through what's left of our army that it is every man for himself. They are to escape if they can, run, hide, whatever, get home if possible." He added, "Find a suitable man to get word to London as fast as he can. Wulfgar, go and find Ealdwine. We must leave now. There are other priests here who can do his work. I want him with me."

I ran off into the gloom to do the King's bidding and, within the hour, a small party of about twenty of us were ready to make a quiet exit from this terrible place.

The moon was waning but still large and thus provided some light for our journey. We feared the Danes would attack us so we headed north, away from their camp – away from London. We followed the river Bourn and then the Granta. One of the Ely monks was from the locality and he helped us to find our way across country and across the Cam. By the time the sun came up, we were on an old Roman track travelling south-west. In fact, to start with, we asked in a village about the way to London and took a route directly south, but then we crept across country onto this old road.

"Aren't we going to London?" I managed to ask Ealdwine.

"Not on this road," he answered. "I think the King is trying to cover our tracks. The Danes will expect us to retreat to the capital and they'll be pursuing us now the light is up and they can see their way."

"But this will take us on a longer road to London," I argued. "The Danes will get in front of us."

Ealdwine glanced at me with a half smile.

"What lies south-west, Wulfgar?"

"I don't know."

"Deerhurst."

I knew why that was important!

"Besides the obvious attractions of that place," the priest continued, "there is the possibility of raising the fyrd in an area that has not contributed to the army before. Fresh troops, that's what the King needs."

I thought he needed a miracle, an army of angels. We had lost huge numbers of thegns, leaders who inspired a loyal following. Perhaps Ealdwine was right and the western area of England and the borders with Wales could provide a new army with which the King could fight for his realm. But I didn't feel optimistic. I don't think any of us did, as much of our journey was in silence.

We found refreshment at a homestead which hadn't been ravaged by recent incursions by the Danes and where the householder was a loyal Englishman. He'd lie if anyone asked whether our party had passed that way, but someone could see us and might tell the Danes, if a dagger was put to their throat. We could not linger long.

We eventually reached Oxford. The leaders there grieved with us over our losses and did what they could to provide refreshment and provisions, but the King was anxious to press on. We knew that by now the Danes would realise we were not heading for London. Their key objective would be to overwhelm us before we could find fresh troops. Oxford had provided men only recently, indeed some of their fyrd had been among those who'd drowned at Brentford so there was no real possibility of raising a serious force here. Further west – Ealdwine was right – that area had not been tapped.

I'll never forget the scene when we arrived at last at Deerhurst. Everyone came running into the yard, shouting the news their lord was here. The hens scattered and the dogs started barking. Lady Frida appeared in the doorway of the hall, her expression a mixture of joy and fear.

"My lord!" she cried and ran towards him as he hurriedly dismounted.

He clasped her in his arms and began to weep. The rest of us dismounted in a more leisurely way, entrusting our horses to the many servants who had poured into the yard. Then we stood quietly waiting. The lady was weeping too by now.

"Terrible losses," I heard him stutter.

"You're alive," she choked. "God has spared you.

261

You'll fight again."

They clung to each other and slowly their shuddering bodies were stilled.

"My lord," she whispered, "come and see your son."

She led him into the hall and the rest of us dispersed so I did not see that moment when the King saw his heir for the first time. By the time I saw them together, he was smiling and more relaxed, cradling his tiny son in his arms, a very proud father.

We were enjoying the food and beginning to talk more after our long and tense journey, but the King interrupted us.

"Men, we cannot stay here," he announced. "We must get across the Severn and put the river between us and the Danes. Then I'll send out to raise the fyrd. Until I have fresh troops, we are vulnerable."

Most of the bodyguard nodded – these men knew about war. I looked across at the lady Frida, whose gaze was on her husband. He had come – what joy! But he brought danger with him. If the Danes caught us, they'd kill the King, his wife and his child. He was putting their lives at risk, but who could blame him for coming here? I didn't! Within hours, therefore, we had crossed the mighty river and found another homestead where we were welcomed. The word went out to the local thegns to provide fighting men, but we feared the Danes would reach us first. We were all surprised by what happened next.

CHAPTER 31

We had been in our new location for about three days, when our meal together in the hall was interrupted. One of the farm workers brought in a visitor on whose arm he had a strong grip.

"I found him," he announced. "He says he has a message."

All eyes turned on the man – a thin, shabby priest.

"Well, well," the King began, "if it isn't Alkmund. What shady deal have you come to make this time?"

"I come from Cnut," he whimpered.

"Cnut?! Changed your master have you?" the King scoffed. "Or is your master still that rat Eadric, but he now serves the enemy of England?"

Alkmund lowered his head. I almost felt sorry for him. How could any man be proud to serve the treacherous earl of Mercia?

"Cnut wishes to parley," he muttered.

There was a stunned silence.

"Parley?" the King asked after a while. "You expect me to believe that? He wants me dead, then he can grab my kingdom."

"I assure you I am sent by Cnut."

The King paused and looked at the wizened specimen before him.

"I will not say yes or no," he responded. "Return tomorrow with Thorkell the Tall and I will consider this proposal. He is to come without a weapon, for I guarantee his safety."

He looked around at all of us.

"You hear me," he commanded. "No one is to harm Thorkell if he comes. No one. You swear?"

"We swear," we chorused.

"Alkmund, you have heard me and my men. Thorkell can come in safety. One of my men speaks Norse so we don't need an interpreter. Just the two of you. You understand?"

"I understand."

"And you agree?"

"I agree."

"See him safely back to the river," the King ordered, and Alkmund was escorted out.

No one spoke straightaway, then subdued conversation resumed, all of us, I think, utterly amazed that Cnut might want to talk. Surely he had enough men to come across the river and crush us, for the local fyrd had not yet gathered.

The next day we gathered round our lord, for we had no intention of leaving him alone with the formidable Thorkell.

Before midday, the two men arrived, the Dane dwarfing the Mercian priest, confident and fearless. He only had our word that we wouldn't harm him, but he had known King Edmund for many years and, I believe, knew him to be a man of honour – unlike the earl of Mercia!

"Greetings, Thorkell," the King announced. "Please sit, both of you."

The great man eased himself down onto a bench. He, too, looked as though he had come through Assandun unscathed.

"You bring us a message from Cnut," the King continued. "There is one here who can translate for us."

A very blonde man stood up and then put the King's words into Thorkell's language. The Dane nodded and the translator reported his reply.

"My leader sends his greetings," Thorkell began. "He says too many men have already died and he suggests a meeting between you and him. Only you and him – with a translator, for his English is limited."

"What would we talk about?" the King enquired.

"He has in mind a solution to this strife, but he has not told me what that is."

"And how does he propose this could happen?"

"We Danes have a tradition of using islands for important meetings," Thorkell explained. "It is proposed that you and he meet on an island in the river. There is one near here called Olney."

"Just Cnut and I?"

"And someone to translate." Thorkell waved his hand at the blonde man. "My leader may accept your man or he may say you should each have a translator. No one would carry any weapons."

"Of course," the King confirmed.

He looked the Dane straight in the eye and Thorkell returned his gaze, almost unblinking. These two understood each other – and respected each other – that much was clear.

"I agree to this meeting," he announced. "In the meantime, no hostilities. Agreed?"

Thorkell nodded.

When he had gone, there was silence; then the King spoke.

"If I refused to meet him, there would only be the option of fighting," he declared. "I have to pursue a path of peace if that is possible."

One of his bodyguards piped up.

"He may suggest resolving the leadership of our country by single combat. That's the sort of thing they do."

The King looked at him and then smiled.

"And who'd win that?" he asked.

"You, sire, of course," was the reply.

"No." He shook his head. "We cannot be so sure. Indeed I've never met him, never seen him fight. I may be some five or so years older and more experienced, but it would be dangerous to be too confident. I will see what he has in mind. I'm not in a position to drive a hard bargain."

That was the truth of it. We'd lost at Assandun and Cnut had the upper hand. The future was bleak.

A couple of days later, the meeting took place. We

English were on the west bank and could see the Danes on the east. Between us lay the small mid-river island of Olney. King Edmund wore only a tunic and leggings and the person I thought was Cnut was similarly attired.

This was the first time I'd had a leisurely view of the Danish leader, as the only other time I'd seen him was when lord Edward tried to kill him. He had fair hair and a close-trimmed beard. He was about the same height as the King, but more slender. I reckoned if he did suggest single combat, he'd lose! But perhaps, even if he'd had that in mind, he might decide against it when he saw the King's muscles and physique.

The blonde man took the King over to the island in a small boat and Cnut with his translator came across to meet them. They made clear to each other that none of them had any weapons and then they sat to parley.

Of course, we couldn't hear what was said and it was difficult to guess from their body language, for the translation process slowed everything up and the meaning of any arm gestures was lost.

"Do you think they might fight it out, Father?" I asked Ealdwine.

"I don't know, but I don't think so," he responded. "There is too much to lose. The rumour is that Cnut has real respect for our King. He admired how he fought so bravely at Assandun, especially after earl Eadric's defection."

"Where is he, by the way?"

"Eadric?"

"Yes."

"I don't know that either," the priest answered. "But I think he must be in the Danish camp. After all, it was his priest who brought the message."

"So he's switched sides again," was my angry response.

"Wulfgar, one day he will have to face the Lord Almighty and give an account of his conduct. God will see through his sweet words."

I thought for a while and then asked him something that had been troubling me.

"Father, the Ely monks brought relics and everyone prayed we'd win," I began, "but we lost and huge numbers of people died, including many fine men. Why did God let the Danes win?"

"That is a hard question," Ealdwine replied. "I have thought about it too and have struggled to find an answer. Indeed, I don't think there is one. Our cause was just, Cnut was the aggressor. God should have been on our side. But we know the good die young, those in the right do not always triumph and evildoers appear to flourish."

He was quiet for a while.

"There is a deep mystery in suffering," he continued. "We do not understand it. Christ suffered terribly, yet his death brought great blessing in the end. We do not always see such good come from *our* suffering."

He looked at me and sighed.

"All I will add," he said, "is that those who do evil will face judgment ultimately. And ... and God does not always intervene in human affairs, even when asked to. That is at the heart of the doctrine of free will. God has left us to make decisions and does not exercise control over us."

"And now our King is faced with a decision," I commented.

"I'm praying he will be wise," the priest admitted, "but he is in a very poor bargaining position. He has called out the fyrd, but even if they came now, we could not defeat Cnut's army. They are formidable fighters and they have the taste of conquest in their mouths."

We had to wait more than an hour before we knew the outcome of the meeting. We saw the two leaders stand and I held my breath. Then they embraced! Some deal had been done – the fighting was over.

The King and Cnut each returned to their forces and I saw the Danes move back from the riverside. We English returned to the homestead and gathered in the hall, anxiously waiting for a report, but the King was in no hurry. He sat silent for several minutes, his shoulders hunched, his head down. Then he looked up and let his eyes fall on each of us in turn.

"Cnut has driven a hard bargain," he reported, "but I was in no position to complain. I have accepted his terms. The fighting is over."

No one spoke. We knew we had lost. I suddenly

remembered how King Aethelred had been forced to flee to Normandy. Perhaps the deal with Cnut included exile for our King! I began to tremble.

"We will pay the Danes tribute; they have demanded ... a very high price for peace," he continued. "We will also exchange hostages to ensure we stick to the bargain."

Hostages! I saw again the mutilated face of Aethelwine and knew what Cnut did to hostages if a deal failed.

"But Cnut wants a quiet life," the King said. "He does not want me kicking my heels in exile and stirring up trouble abroad. He would rather I was kept busy at home."

I had no idea what he meant. It sounded as though he wouldn't be exiled, but how would he be 'kept busy'?

"He has granted me Wessex. I am to be King of Wessex and he will be King of the rest of England."

There was a great intake of breath across the hall, but no one had a chance to comment, for the King suddenly stood up and disappeared into his private room where no doubt the lady Frida was waiting to comfort him. We were left speechless.

King of Wessex! Like King Alfred, I thought. Not since his time had the kingdom been divided. It was a bitter blow, but ... but, as I thought about it, surely it was better than exile.

The next day, the King sought me out.

"Wulfgar, come with me across the river," he ordered.

"I want to show my son the church at Deerhurst."

In fact, several small boats crossed the Severn, for his bodyguard came too – the agreement made had yet to be sealed by money and the exchange of hostages.

He made me carry his sword, while he carried the child in his arms.

"I cannot enter the house of God with a sword at my side," he explained, "but I need to feel it is not far from my grip if I need it."

I nodded and trotted behind him to the church. The bodyguard stayed outside, while at the entrance, the King paused.

"You see these beast heads, Edward," he said to the tiny boy, "how bright they are painted. That is to scare away the devil."

He chuckled and the little one smiled back and gurgled happily.

"And here is the Virgin to whom this church is dedicated."

He crossed himself and let his eyes rest on the stone-carved figure.

"She carries within her the Christ child," he explained, "the hope of all the world – and still our hope, our strength."

He touched Edward's head with some holy water from the stoop by the door and touched his own forehead too. I followed his example before walking behind them into the great church, which smelt of incense and had a cool peace pervading it. He paused at the font.

"Here you were named, my son. I'm sorry I wasn't here for your baptism, but the Danes have kept me busy since before your birth. You have the name of your great uncle Edward and of other kings in your lineage. We have fine ancestors, you and I, and among them was King Alfred who fought Norsemen too. He was pushed to the margins of his kingdom and hid in the watery places of Somerset. But he emerged stronger and more determined and he drove back the Norse and eventually his children returned England to the English."

He began to wander towards the high altar. Candles burned in many alcoves, their light mixing with the sunbeams that pushed through the narrow windows. He knelt before the cross and I sensed he was praying. The child was quiet in his arms, his eyes fixed on the face of his father.

As the King rose from his knees, I heard him say, "Edward, your descendants will be kings of England. This is not the end. It is but a new beginning."

E N D S

If you have enjoyed this book, please email the author at fenflack@btinternet.com.

Historical note

The facts of Edmund's life are, for the most part, recorded in the Anglo-Saxon Chronicle which exists, for this period, in three versions. I have not strayed from the recorded facts, but I have interpreted them sometimes and filled in the gaps.

It is known that he married the widow of Siferth, who is also called Sigeferth (I chose the simpler version of his name). Only one chronicler names this lady as Ealdgyth. However, that was definitely the name of Morcar's wife, as she is named in a will. Whilst it is possible the brothers had married women with the same name, it has been suggested the chronicler has got them muddled. In the light of this doubt and to avoid confusion, I have given her the completely fictitious name of Frida.

We know that Edmund's wife gave birth to two sons and some scholars have suggested she had twins. I have stuck to single births. There is also some disagreement about whether Edward was the younger or older child. He is named first before his brother by John of Worcester and so I have made him the elder. As his place of birth is unknown, I have chosen Deerhurst – and why not?!

Wulfstan, Bishop of Worcester and Archbishop of York, wrote what is called the "Sermon of the Wolf to the English". As this work was probably first preached in 1014 before being circulated in manuscript form, I have him working on a draft when visited by Edmund and

Wulfgar late in 1013. I have then used parts of it as his Candlemas sermon in 1014. The translation is from Dorothy Whitelock's "English Historical Documents" Vol. 1 (London, 1979). A full script of Athelstan's will can also be found there.

The attack by Edmund's young half-brother, Edward, is found in the Icelandic saga called *Flateyarbok*. It is somewhat improbable and it may be Edmund is the person meant rather than Edward, but I've gone with it being real because it's such a good addition to the novel.

The site of Assandun is disputed, both Ashdon in north-west Essex and Ashingdon in south-east Essex claiming to be where the battle took place. I have chosen to locate the battle in Ashdon.

Fen Flack